THE SECRET
OF THE
MEZUZAH

PASSPORT TO DANGER · BOOK ONE

THE SECRET OF THE MEZUZAH

MARY REEVES BELL

BETHANY HOUSE PUBLISHERS
MINNEAPOLIS, MINNESOTA 55438

The Secret of the Mezuzah
Revised edition 1999
Copyright © 1995, 1999
Mary Reeves Bell

Cover illustration by Cheri Bladholm
Cover design by the Lookout Design Group

This book is a work of fiction. The historical backdrop is accurate, however, and Austrian president Kurt Waldheim, Maria Rozstoski, Nazi officer Gustav Richter, and Simon Wiesenthal are indeed real people. Although the events surrounding him in this story are purely fictional, Wiesenthal is a survivor of the Holocaust who has spent his life in the pursuit of justice. He continues to live and work in Vienna, Austria, seeking to track down Nazi war criminals. Other stories and characters are fictitious. Any resemblance to people living or dead is coincidental.

Published by Bethany House Publishers
A Ministry of Bethany Fellowship International
11400 Hampshire Avenue South
Minneapolis, Minnesota 55438
www.bethanyhouse.com

Printed in the United States of America by
Bethany Press International, Minneapolis, Minnesota 55438

ISBN 1–55661–549–3

For Eugene Constantine Bell—

my firstborn

MARY REEVES BELL spent six years as a missionary in Austria. While there she specialized in Hebrew and Hebraic studies at the University of Vienna and developed an interest in keeping the memory of the Holocaust alive. Mary frequently travels to Romania, where she works with abandoned children. She and her husband, David, have three sons and currently live in Virginia.

CONTENTS

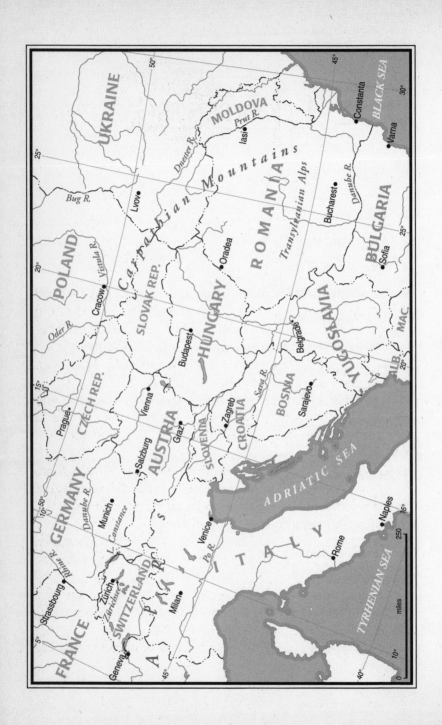

THE BAKERY

I SHOULDN'T HAVE STOPPED IN THE BAKERY THAT DAY.

I shouldn't have. But I did.

The wind blew a blast of cold air down my neck as I started down Braungasse. I pulled up my collar to shut out the cold and looked across the street at the bakery. I was late already because of heavy traffic in the narrow road through the Vienna Woods, but I didn't want to go home yet and face Mom with the note stuffed in my backpack.

Besides, my mom was not big on after-school snacks, and the thought of Branko's fresh-baked goodies was too much. Giving in to my stomach, I started across the street—and then I saw it.

Hey, hey, hey, I thought, whistling under my breath, *that's what I call a car*. In front of the bakery sat a red E-type Jaguar with its motor idling. Exhaust from its powerful engine sprayed leaves down the gutter in a steady stream.

A 1972—3.8 liter—V-12 engine! And in perfect condition, too. What a beauty of a beast! I stood still, drooling over the great old sports car.

Despite the cold wind, the driver had his bare arm hanging out the open window, tapping his hand against the door to vibrations from the car radio.

What a jerk, I thought. The guy was a skinhead with a big

tattoo on his forearm. I was too far away to make it out for sure, but it looked like a swastika. Heavy metal music poured into the street.

It was weird to see his type in our quiet neighborhood. In the center of the city and on the tram, Hannah and I had seen skinheads. We never admitted it to each other, but they were scary and we always kept our distance from them.

As much as I would've liked to, I wasn't about to walk up and ask to look in the car. Before the driver noticed me staring and decided to smash my face in, a fair-skinned, well-dressed man carrying a leather briefcase walked out of Branko's bakery and got in on the passenger side.

Show's over, I thought and stepped into the street. The engine growled as the driver shoved it in gear. At that moment a branch loosened by last night's storm came down in a crash, glanced off my back, and knocked me in the path of the Jag.

He swerved to miss me, barely succeeding, and screeched to a stop. As I rolled over and sat up, scratched but not seriously hurt, the driver backed up far enough to get around me, then sped off shaking his fist and swearing—I'm sure—but in a totally unrecognizable language.

"And may you grow hair all over your ugly skinhead," I said to his red tail as it disappeared around the corner at the bottom of the hill. I could see it narrowly miss a tram as he turned off of Braungasse into the heavy traffic of Wahringerstrasse.

I looked around to see if anyone had witnessed my humiliation. But as usual, all was quiet, and I brushed off the rest of the foliage, thankful for the thick leather of my jacket. I continued, carefully, across the street.

The bell above the entrance jangled wildly as the wind slammed the door shut behind me. Warmth and the smell of freshly baked bread filled the tiny front room of the bakery.

"Gruss dich, Constantine," Branko bellowed as he came out of the kitchen behind the pastry case. Although German was neither his nor my first language, we both spoke it fluently.

"Gruss dich, Branko," I replied, looking in vain for a Berliner and hoping he had remembered to save me one or two of my favorite jelly-filled doughnuts. Berliners were one of the few things I loved about Vienna. Maybe the only thing.

I pulled off my backpack and slung it onto "my table" by the door. The palms of my hands burned from the fall, and I brushed the leaves and bits of gravel out of the skinned parts. *What a jerk*, I thought again. *That guy could have killed me.*

"Who's the foreigner?" I asked, still nursing my hands. "His friend nearly ran over me in that red Jag."

"Never seen him before," Branko said, rather unconcerned, I thought, about my brush with death. "What makes you think he wasn't Austrian?"

"Branko—his driver swore at me! I've been sworn at in German, and that wasn't German. The guy practically runs over me, then yells as if it's my fault. He could've killed me."

Branko ignored my theatrics and answered with his dry humor. "The gentleman who came in spoke perfectly polite German to me. However, it is possible he does not like tall, skinny fifteen-year-old boys who fall into his path."

"Lean, Branko, lean—not skinny. Get it right. And I didn't fall—I was hit by the stupid tree. He might have been a gentleman, but his driver definitely wasn't. Okay?"

"Okay." He laughed. "Whatever you say. I think now you could use a little refreshment. How about joining me in a snack?"

He always said that. And I always did.

Waiting for Branko to join me, I inspected the damage to my backpack. I was surprised to see the branch had ripped right through the material, tearing off the emblem that said *American International School, Vienna, Austria*. Rubbing the emblem gently, I thought, *Better it than my right shoulder.*

Everything inside the pack seemed to be intact, including, regrettably, the note from pain-in-the-neck Gaul. It was a sealed and bring-back-a-response kind of note. Hard to open and get away with it. I sighed. It probably said the usual: *Constantine is not living up to his potential.* I could be certain of one thing: It wasn't a compliment on my school performance. And removing it for rewriting was probably not possible without the help of Hannah, who with time could forge anything. A short, bumpy bus ride wasn't long enough, she had assured me on the way home.

"What are you thinking about?" Branko asked as he joined me, bringing a mug full of cold cider for me and a plate of Berliners for both of us.

"Are you up to no good again?" he asked. "I know that look of yours; it has earned you your nickname I think, Con, my boy."

"Not a chance," I said, biting into the soft, powdery pastry and licking the red raspberry jam that squeezed out onto my fingers.

"Not a chance you're not, if I know you. Your handsome face may impress Hannah and all your other girlfriends; however, I happen to know it conceals a very sneaky brain," he said as he leaned back in his chair and observed me devouring the Berliner.

"Ha. A lot you know. Hannah is not, as you put it, my girlfriend. She is a friend who just happens to be a girl. It's like . . . a coincidence."

"Oh, I see," Branko said smiling. "Thanks for clarifying that. She's a very pretty coincidence."

We enjoyed our Berliners together, and I amused him with incidents from another day in the life of a student.

He always listened to me. A bakery is usually quiet in late afternoon since most daily shopping is completed in the morning. I had been visiting Branko since the week we moved into this neighborhood, and he always seemed glad to see me.

It occurred to me—not for the first time—that Branko Lov-eric, my friendly baker, did not look like one at all. For one thing he was too big. Not fat like old Fritz, the last owner, but just really, really big. Fritz was so fat he died of a heart attack and fell right into the pumpernickel dough he was kneading—or so they say.

No way Branko's going to end up in any batch of dough, I thought. In fact, he looked more like a bouncer than a baker. Except for his eyes. They rested on you kindly, unoccupied else-where. Still, I was glad he was friend not foe.

"Thanks," I said, wiping the powdered sugar off my face. "That was great. I'd probably starve to death without you."

"I doubt it" was his cynical response.

"No—I'm not kidding. My mom's into gourmet cooking now, trying to make fancy meals for dinner every night. Show-ing off for Nigel."

"That is bad?" he asked.

"Let me put it this way. Let's hope Nigel didn't marry her for her cooking, or this is going to be a short marriage."

Branko had a kind of suppressed laughter you didn't hear so much as see. His whole body shook, which made the little wooden chair beneath him creak dangerously.

"She's never bothered with fancy cooking before," I went on. "Now instead of normal hamburgers we have rare rabbit drowned in red wine or something equally inedible."

"I'm sure she will improve with time," he said. "And in the meantime, you can come here for emergency rations."

"Thanks. But I wish she had just stuck to her usual pursuits, which are already strange enough."

"Like what?"

"Like what? Like how many mothers do you know—Americans to boot—who study Hebrew at the University of Vienna?"

Branko looked at me like I might have a point.

"That is a little unusual, I admit," he said. "Why does she?"

"Who knows? She's always studying or writing something or other. Hebrew is only the latest thing. She actually enjoys studying. I didn't inherit the urge." I groaned at the reminder and told him what I thought the note from Ms. Gaul was about.

" 'Constantine, if you don't bring out those well-concealed brains of yours and get to work, you will not make it in my class.' " I mimicked Ms. Gaul perfectly, right down to the jerking of the head.

He chuckled. "The question is, do you have any brains to bring out?"

"Ha!" I snorted. "It wouldn't be worth the effort in her class. And besides, she has no sense of humor. Hannah thinks her problem is tight hair."

"Tight hair?" Branko looked really confused at that one.

"Yeah, you know, on her head. She pulls her hair back in a tight little knot until her eyes become thin slits."

I leaned forward, resting my head on the rim of the empty apple cider mug. The thought of that woman was too much to bear.

"If only Mom would have let me live in the States—even for part of the year. It would be great at my grandparents' ranch. I'm tired of Vienna, tired of humorless teachers and their stupid notes," I said dramatically.

"Con—Con, you are a little bit crazy. Humorless teachers are a widespread problem, found in every country in the world. And I cannot imagine your mother, or Nigel for that matter, without you. Even for a few months. Besides, Vienna is a very exciting city. Your American cousins probably envy you very much living here."

"Oh sure," I said sarcastically. "No baseball, one measly McDonald's, no TV worth watching. Sure they do."

Just then the door of the bakery opened, and in came our

landlady and monumental pain: Frau Schnively.

She smiled at me, a plump, disapproving little smile, and said, "Constantine Rea, you should be home, dear. School was over ages ago. Your mother will be worried."

Nosy busybody. My mom wasn't the worrying type.

Frau Schnively always seemed to be shivering slightly, pulling her layers of sweaters tightly over her not too tiny chest. Whether she was cold or forever disgusted with things around her, I wasn't too sure. Probably the latter. She reminded me of a fat little chicken, clucking and fluttering about, pecking her nose in other people's business.

Funny seeing her in Branko's bakery, I thought while I watched him wait on her. She was always warning my mom about shopping here: "You can't trust a foreigner, you know. And that man can't be expected to make Viennese pastry like a true Viennese."

To which my mother always reasonably pointed out to her, "The man has lived in Vienna since he was six years old, for heaven's sake." But as Mom says, Frau Schnively is not one to allow reason to interfere with her prejudices.

I turned my eyes and mind away from her and considered what Branko had just said about Vienna being an exciting city. It didn't look like it from where I was sitting. The wind continued to blow the leaves about on Braungasse—a boring old street in a tired old city. Although I had lived in Austria all my life, we had recently moved to Vienna. Probably nothing exciting had happened here for hundreds of years. Now, my ideal of an exciting city was Malibu, California. And in the immortal words of someone, maybe me, Vienna was no Malibu.

Mom always bragged that Braungasse wasn't a tourist trap. *Maybe not*, I thought miserably. *But it sure is a trap*.

Huge stone houses lined the street, each with a fenced-in yard and sturdy, locked metal gates. Home is where your fortress is in this neighborhood, and ours was down the hill from

Branko's bakery, only one block from the number 48 tramline stop.

Take it for forty-five Schillings with one transfer and you could go anywhere in Vienna. Which is what Hannah and I had been doing lately for entertainment. We would ride the tram on Saturday afternoon until we spotted a likely "criminal type," then follow him until he noticed us or we got bored waiting for him to commit an exciting criminal act. We hoped in vain. Other than dirty looks and a few colorful German words, we came up with zip.

Frau Schnively finally left the bakery with her "inferior goods" and superior attitude. Tugging at her layers of gray sweaters as the wind hit her, she scurried down the street as if she had somewhere important to go.

"How old were you when your father died?" Branko startled me by asking as he sat back down. He had refilled my mug with cold cider. I took a big swig before answering and wondered why he had asked that all of a sudden.

"It was before I was born," I said, thinking about all the years of wishing for a dad. I realized I had pretty much gotten over it. And now, after all those years, Mom had married Nigel. . . .

"I am sorry," he said simply. We were both quiet for a moment.

"He was a military pilot, you know," I told him proudly.

"Hmm. Something to be proud of," Branko said, looking at me kindly.

"Not really," I replied, telling the truth about it for once. "He wasn't killed in combat, fighting some great war for freedom. He was 'killed in maneuvers.' Whatever that means."

I used to take the letter from the air force out of Mom's desk and read it over and over, wondering how it happened. It made it worse that he was killed for nothing. Dead without glory.

"You know," Branko said, "wars are never great, Con.

Some are just more necessary, that's all."

"If he had to die, I wish he could have died a hero," I insisted.

It embarrassed me to think of all the times I had lied about his death by making it a heroic thing.

Branko sensed my discomfort. "In my experience it is more often how people live that makes them heroic than how they die."

I didn't know what to say. True or not, the image I had of my dad was of a soldier dying for his country. How could I ever think of someone like Nigel as my dad? A quiet businessman never doing anything dangerous or heroic?

"You know," Branko continued, "I don't remember my father, either. He was killed during World War II, in 1944. I was the youngest of five boys. It must have been terrible for my mother. She could scarcely find enough food to feed us. But she managed, and after the war she married an Austrian and we moved from our little village, in what was then Yugoslavia, here to Vienna. It really is a nice city, Con. You will get used to it—and to having a father. I did."

Nigel had entered our lives about one year ago when he and Mom had been stranded in London's Heathrow Airport, both waiting for the same flight back to Vienna. They discovered their mutual love of old, rare books and out-of-the-way used bookstores. *Thrilling*, I had thought when Mom excitedly told me about this wonderful man she had just met who actually spent some of his free time in the same bookstores she did. *Now, that's the kind of man I can relate to*, I thought with sarcasm when he came over for his first visit. But I cheered up considerably when he took us for a drive in his new car.

"Oh, it's not that Nigel isn't all right," I explained to Branko. "He's nice enough . . . and there is the BMW. Man, can he drive that car!"

Branko shook his head and rolled his eyes upward.

"But you're wrong about Vienna. Nothing exciting ever happens here," I insisted.

"Con, Con, Con," he said in mock exasperation. "Exciting things are happening all the time, only you don't see it. Vienna is still the hub of international espionage. One out of every ten adults in Vienna is a spy working for someone or other."

Spies? Here? I began to get that same tingling feeling I get when Nigel is crashing along some twisting mountain road in the BMW. I sat up straight in my chair.

"Why Vienna? And there aren't spies anymore. Remember, the Cold War ended and all that?"

"Oh, you are wrong, my boy. There are still many spies. The KGB still exists; so does the CIA, for that matter. There are men and women who once worked as spies for the communists, and now they are looking for new masters. There is industrial espionage. There are terrorists and those they pay for information. And there is always the danger of war in this region."

His voice changed as he went on. "Right in my dear country of Yugoslavia, which was destroyed by civil war while Europe stood by watching. Serbian forces destroyed the village where I was born. All the Croatian people had to flee, including my brothers and their families. And do not think for one moment that all of us have given up our land and our country and are quietly moving on."

Anger had transformed my friendly baker, but he seemed to check himself and return to his easy manner. I thought again of the man who had left the shop. Without any goods! I just remembered that. Why would anyone go into a bakery and leave empty-handed? And no matter what Branko said, that crazy man in the Jag had not been speaking German. It could have been Serbian, though—or Branko's native Croatian tongue, which is very similar.

Branko continued speaking. "And don't forget Vienna is

still the gateway to the Middle East. And you know from Hannah about the trouble that persists between Arabs and Israelis. Open your eyes, Con, there is still much going on inside Vienna's ancient walls. New hatreds and old."

He wasn't kidding about the spies, although he clearly wanted me to stop thinking about his outburst about Yugoslavia. I was beginning to like Vienna more by the minute.

"What are the spies all doing?"

"Ordinary kinds of things. That is their cover." He leaned over the table, all intense. "It is what you don't see that is interesting. Chances are"—he tapped my chest with his finger—"you know someone right now, see them nearly every day, and don't know their true identity. You see, Con," he said, switching to English, "there are spies amongst us."

Branko had learned English from British soldiers stationed in Vienna after the war. He would laugh at my cool American expressions, and I'd laugh at his old-fashioned British ones.

" 'Spies amongst us,' Branko? Oh sure!"

My skepticism showed, but he smiled knowingly and said no more. The anger had gone out of his eyes. Maybe I had imagined it.

"I don't know of any spies 'amongst' me. Still, I wish you were my World History teacher," I said, thinking of the alternative. "Or any of my teachers, for that matter."

"Sorry, but I don't think your fancy private school would have me. What would I teach? I know only baking and judo."

I looked at him, startled. "Judo?" I couldn't believe it. "Why didn't you tell me before? Would you give me some lessons some time? What about next week?"

"Maybe. Maybe. Calm down," he said. "It is really nothing." That last bit had evidently slipped out.

My mind leaped to make the obvious connection. It would also explain the man in the Jag. I knew it. There was something wrong about that whole thing. Branko had a secret life. The quiet baker was a front, and today I had seen his contact.

"Why does a baker need to know judo anyway?" I asked, trying not to sound suspicious.

He looked into my eyes all serious like and hesitated, considering his words carefully. *He's going to tell me, take me into his confidence and admit he is a spy. Maybe even recruit me.* My heart pounded.

"Yes—yes," I urged him on.

"Well . . . we have to get out of a lot of sticky situations."

"Give me a break," I groaned as he leaned back in his chair, enjoying his little joke. "Sticky situations—like sticky buns? Weak, Branko. Weak." I wasn't fooled.

"Do you really know judo, with a black belt and all that?"

"Yes, but let's just keep that between ourselves." His stern expression and serious voice made it a command.

"Sure, if you say so." I was really wondering now.

"Get yourself going, Con. I don't want your mom to worry." Branko moved his large frame off of the chair and, moving more quickly now, took our things behind the counter. He seemed in a hurry for me to go all of a sudden.

I wiped the powdered sugar from my hands and stood up, putting on my new leather flight jacket. I had been wanting one for ages, and Grandma had sent it right before school started. It had saved my skin this afternoon when the branch fell on me. I pulled my Oakley sunglasses from an inside pocket, relieved to find them undamaged.

"Great," I said out loud, thankful they had been protected by the thick layers of leather when I fell. I put them on, ready to face the music at home.

"Look out for yourself, kid," Branko said conspiratorially as I opened the door to go. "You never know who might be watching you. Frau Schnively could be an agent for a foreign power."

The thought of the very proper Frau Schnively leading a

double life affected us both the same way. Hysterically.

The door jingled as it closed, knocking the little bell hanging over it back and forth. I waved to Branko through the window and glanced up at the trees.

I couldn't see anything else ready to drop on me, so I swung the damaged backpack over my shoulder and started confidently down the street. What a day. New, exciting possibilities were opening up to me, thanks to Branko. I was seeing Vienna in a totally different light. And thinking he had revealed much more about himself than he meant to, I walked down Braungasse, very happy with the plan already forming in my brain.

2

A SPY AMONGST US

Searching through my pockets for my key to get into our fortified courtyard, I came up empty. As usual I had forgotten it. Rather than irritate Frau Schnively, who frowned on my scaling the wall, I pushed the button marked *49A* on the stone side post and heard it buzz inside.

Mom looked out the kitchen window, saw it was me, and released the three locks necessary to get me through the outer courtyard and into our apartment. Austrians are highly suspicious people. Especially Frau Schnively, who would have a fit if she discovered we had extra sets of keys. We hid them in strategic locations, as we seemed to lose ours on a regular basis. I had even given Hannah a set—just in case of an emergency.

It's a good thing I did, too. I pushed open our heavy wooden front door. Hannah's assistance would be critical to pull off my plan. She was going to love this. Good ol' Branko had given me more than Berliners today. I would tell her about it tomorrow. In the meantime, I'd run it past Mom. Part of it, that is.

"Come into the kitchen; I'm making dinner," she called as I threw my things on the hall table.

I had decided on the way home to be cool and wait for the best moment to bring out the note, probably after dinner. *If tonight's gourmet meal is a hit*, I thought, *Mom will be in a good mood. On the other hand . . .* Oh well, better later than now.

I pulled myself up and sat on the counter. "Hi, Mom."

"Hi yourself, Con. You were certainly long enough at the bakery this afternoon. I suppose you ruined your appetite again."

"That's not what ruins it," I said without thinking.

"What do you mean by that?" Her tone suggested I had not answered wisely.

"Nothing. Not a thing. What's for dinner tonight, anyway?"

"Wiener Schnitzel, gemischtes Gemüse, and Petersilie Kartoffel," she said rather proudly.

"Gemischte ge-what? Let's go eat at the Wienerwald."

"My Schnitzel will be even better," she said looking at me. "And if you are as smart as I think you are, you won't even be tempted to touch that with one of your cute remarks."

"Not with a ten-foot pole," I agreed. She was kidding, but underneath the kidding Mom seemed tense and preoccupied.

Lowering my voice and leaning close to her for effect, I said, "There is a spy amongst us."

"What?" Mom asked in that absentminded way that tells you she doesn't care if you answer.

I answered her anyway, using Branko's phrase again. "There is a spy amongst us. And I was almost run over by one coming out of the bakery today."

Mom went on making the Schnitzel. She was being especially thorough about pounding the meat paper-thin.

"You look okay to me," she said, totally unconcerned.

Persevering, I went on with this rather one-sided conversation. "One out of every ten people in Vienna is a spy for someone or other."

"That's fascinating," Mom said, continuing to pound. "Where did you pick up that important bit of information? School?"

"Of course not. The information you pick up at school is

rarely important. Branko told me."

"Well, a Croatian baker is undoubtedly an expert on spy quotas," she said sarcastically. "I would take his word for it if I were you."

"I did. Who do you think it is?"

"Who do I think who is?" she asked, still pounding away.

At her present rate of attack, the Wiener Schnitzel would soon be ground to dust. *Maybe she's mad at Nigel,* I thought cheerfully. It would be nice having someone to share her bad moods.

"Mom," I shouted over the pounding, "would you stop beating the poor thing to death and listen to me? This is important. I know more than ten adults here in Vienna, so it stands to reason that one of them is a spy. And I intend to find out which one."

Mom pointed the mallet at me. "This 'poor thing,' as you refer to it, has been dead for ages. So I can't possibly be beating it to death. Do try to be more accurate, Con. Now, why on earth are you rambling on about spies?"

"I'm going to apply my great reasoning ability to discover a spy. According to Branko's statistics, one of our friends, assuming we have more than ten, has a secret life. A life of danger, daring, excitement, intrigue—stuff like that." I was really getting into this.

"As to your great reasoning ability, it is something heretofore untested, as your grades tend to indicate. And besides, you are misapplying the information received from a statistic."

"Well, it is possible, isn't it, that one of the ten adults I know here in Vienna is a spy?" I argued.

"Yes, of course it is possible. It's possible that Nigel will be home on time for dinner tonight. However, both are highly unlikely!" This was said with a final pounding to the Schnitzel.

"Oh. So that's why you're massacring the meat. Nigel is going to be late again." I knew at once that was a mistake. Red starts on her neck and moves upward when Mom is angry or frustrated. Her face was taking on a rosy glow.

"First of all, I am not 'massacring' the meat." She pounded again for emphasis. "Do I mind if my gourmet meals lose their bloom of youth before they see the light of day?"

Mom tends to mix her metaphors when upset.

"And furthermore," she went on, "only silly, jealous, insecure wives fail to understand when responsibilities make a husband late for dinner. Since I am none of the above, let's drop this conversation. Don't you have some homework to do?"

I decided it was time to leave the room. Mom and I had lived alone a long time, and we understood each other pretty well. I didn't like to see her hurt or upset, but I felt strangely glad knowing that I wasn't the only one in our "flat"—as Nigel called it—still getting used to the new arrangement.

I took my backpack out to the deck so I could watch the cars going up and down Braungasse. The wind had gone down but it was still cool, and I left my leather jacket on. Maybe the beautiful red Jaguar would go by again on its way to Branko's bakery. I knew for certain there was something suspicious going on. But as nothing of interest went by, I actually did all of my homework, then moved on to more interesting things. Like my spy list. I put Branko at the top. As the list got longer, I knew I would need more than Hannah's help to check out the suspects.

Even though Mom didn't like Gregor Müller much—she hated it when I went to his house because she worried about "supervision"—I knew I would need the help of someone who knew his way around Vienna. And in fact the lack of supervision Mom worried about might be a great help to Hannah and me. I couldn't wait to tell Hannah about my plan.

Besides, I reasoned, *Gregor is my only Austrian friend in Vienna, and Mom will just have to get over her worries about his influence on me.* There were no other kids my age in the neighborhood, and I had been lonely when we moved to Braungasse. Gregor had showed up the first week.

That night at dinner, I brought up my spy search again. Things were unusually quiet; the silence had been broken only once so far. Nigel made what he obviously thought to be a perfectly normal compliment. "This certainly is tender Schnitzel," he said, trying in vain to get one whole bite to his mouth before it crumbled off his fork. A warning look from Mom told me to keep my mouth shut.

"So . . . how many people work for you, Nigel?" I asked, quickly changing the subject.

"Let's see," he said. "Here in the Vienna office, about fifty or so. More in the field, of course. I have sales staff in Moscow, Warsaw, Prague, and Budapest, each consisting of five to ten people. Why?"

All those people in his Vienna office and contacts in the old communist countries. I nearly choked on the bite I had taken. *There must be someone*, I thought. *Out of all those people, there must be a spy in Nigel's office, too.*

"Have you ever wondered who your mole is?"

He looked a bit bewildered. "My mole?"

"Yeah."

"Didn't know I had one. Come to think of it, though, my secretary does look a bit like a mole."

"No," I laughed. "A spy. One out of every ten adults in Vienna—"

Mom interrupted me with a groan. "Here we go again."

"Oh, that kind of mole," he said. "Well, to the best of my knowledge, there are no spies in my offices. But then, one never knows with spies, does one?"

"Right. Exactly my point. They are all around us, and we don't even know who they are. I made a list this afternoon of possible suspects. Now it's just a matter of some good detecting, something Hannah and I have been practicing."

"Well, that sounds like a jolly good idea to me, Con. It's better as a pastime than bashing little old ladies in the street and stealing their handbags, I suppose." He looked at Mom, hoping, I think, for a smile. None appeared.

"Homework is probably a more useful pastime, don't you think?" Mom said.

"It's finished," I protested. "So is my spy list, and Branko is definitely at the top." I was dying to tell them he was a judo expert, but I had given my word. I did, however, tell them about the skinhead who nearly ran over me outside the bakery.

"Branko hardly seems a likely candidate," Nigel said.

"Why not? He's very suspicious."

"And what do you suspect him of?" Mom asked, getting into this in spite of herself, her tension disappearing. "Do you think he's passing micro-dots in the poppy seeds, maybe?"

"Espionage eclairs . . . or clandestine cookies," Nigel added. They both laughed. Parents are easily amused.

"Very funny. He's a foreigner, you know."

"So are you," Nigel said. "So are we all."

But when I appealed to Nigel's superior male intellect, he agreed it was possible Branko or someone else we knew could be a spy.

"The trick is finding out who," he said. "Your mother seems mildly shady to me." He gave her a sappy smile. "Are you working secretly for anyone, Roberta?"

Roberta is Mom's full name. All our friends and family call her Berta. When he says Roberta in that terribly upper-class British accent, I'm not sure for a minute who he means.

They laughed. As usual, they didn't take me seriously, but I was glad to see Mom's bad mood gone and decided to drop the subject.

We all carried our dishes into the kitchen and came back with dessert, which Mom had wisely purchased from Branko. I had another glass of milk with the sweet, rich Linzertorte. Mom and Nigel drank a cup of coffee with whipped cream in it, Vienna style.

"Look at this photograph that came in the mail today," Mom said, reaching toward a side table on which stacks of letters and neatly ordered papers stood.

It was a picture taken last spring in the States during our yearly trip to my grandparents' ranch in Wyoming. We had gone right before Mom and Nigel's wedding. In the background you could see Grandma's house—my real home. *Funny that it's Grandma's house, but the barns, corrals, and animals are Grandpa's.*

Grandpa was standing behind the group in the picture. Tall to begin with, his ever present cowboy hat made him tower over us. His kind face was weathered by years in the sun. The smartest and best rancher ever. I missed them both.

Nigel pointed to Grandma. "Looks like a nice lady."

"Yup!" I said. "She looks like a proper little granny, and she is, too. But I remember the day we were out riding together when—lo and behold—who did we run into but the meanest, cheatin'est hombre in those parts." I slipped into western lingo for Nigel's sake. "Old man Marvin. Fred Marvin had been running wild horses on Grandpa's land for years. Well, he says, 'Good morning, madam,' tipping his hat to her—real polite like. She looks him right in the eye and says just as cool as anything, 'It won't be a good morning in this valley until you take your cheating outfit and get out of it.' "

"That's my mom," Mom said, grinning.

"Who are all these girls?" Nigel asked. "Poor Con is the only boy in the group."

"Yes . . . poor Con," Mom said, "with six adoring girl cousins. The fact that he's the only boy helps, plus his slightly European accent and world travels add to his charm. Everyone there rather fawns over him, I'm afraid. Don't you agree, Con?"

" 'Fawns over'? What kind of expression is 'fawns over,' Mom?" I asked. "Sounds like something a deer might do, especially in the spring."

"Weak, Con!" Mom replied, looking very smug. "You know you're not good at word association—or even reading words, for that matter." She started to laugh. "Remember the

'Presbyterians Crossing' sign you saw last summer and read out to the whole car?"

"Oh no," I protested to Nigel. "Do not believe this. She's making this up."

He looked amused and more than a little confused. "Presbyterians crossing? Do they have signs like that in the States outside churches?"

That sent Mom over the edge, collapsing into giggles worse than the girls in my class.

"Oh yes," she said, "they do indeed. Con saw another interesting sign later that said, 'Warning—Heavy Episcopalians Working.' He shared that one with us, too."

"Well . . . heavy Episcopalians working does sound like something to avoid at all costs, probably more dangerous than the typical Heavy Equipment Working. . . ." He gave my arm a light punch. "You have to keep the troops entertained, don't you, boy?"

"Dead right," I said, using Nigel's expression and accent. "Smart chap you married, Mom."

Mom wiped away the tears from laughing so hard, and we stood up. She surprised me with a big hug, kind of urgent like, and said, "Don't grow up too soon. Stay just the way you are, Constantine." Very emotional, that—for my mom.

Right before going to bed, I slipped the note from Ms. Gaul under their door, hoping it wasn't trouble. I was totally unaware that real trouble was more than an irritated teacher and closer than I could have imagined.

3

PRANKS AND PREJUDICE

THE FINAL BELL RANG THROUGH THE HALLS OF THE American International School ten minutes later than usual due to an unscheduled assembly. Another cold fall wind blew down through the Vienna Woods as I ran to catch the bus with Hannah.

"Who do you think did it?" I called over my shoulder, referring to the subject of the hastily called assembly: graffiti sprayed on the school walls. We maneuvered between two limos waiting by the curb. Diplomats' kids from all over the world came to our school. A row of Mercedes with chauffeurs waited for students whose parents were either worried about their safety or too snobby to let them ride a common school bus like the rest of us.

A dark-skinned, bearded man wearing a black uniform and a neat, red turban leaned against one limo and gave us a cool stare as we squeezed past him. I didn't recognize him as one of the usual chauffeurs.

Reva Abdul, a Kuwaiti girl in my math class, smiled slightly at us as she climbed into the next car in line—a very nice maroon stretch job.

"I think she likes me," I said to Hannah while waving at her.

"You think everyone likes you," she answered, unimpressed.

Fascinated by the burly man with a permanent scowl who always picked her up, I asked Reva once if her driver ever got bored waiting for her. "Not driver, bodyguard," she had said blankly. As if it were normal. His face was never warm and friendly, and today the professional gaze he cast over the street and school yard as he closed the door for Reva was cold as ice.

There were more limos than usual—and an air of tension that could only be explained by the trouble at school. Phone calls must have alerted embassies of the "unpleasantness," as the principal had put it.

Crudely drawn swastikas and the English words *Foreigners Out* had been spray-painted in blood red in the boys' bathroom off the gym and on the outside south wall of our secluded private school. Leaflets in German with more of the same message had been scattered around. It happened during fifth period and was discovered as classes changed afterward. Someone had managed to get on campus while class was in session without being noticed.

"Those responsible will soon be caught," a more uptight than usual Principal Miller had assured us during the assembly, his threat increased by the uniformed policeman sitting behind him.

"They don't have a clue," I said to Hannah.

"I know, and it scares me. Swastikas aren't funny to my family," Hannah answered, clearly upset. We climbed onto the mostly empty bus and sat in the back.

"Racists," she said, looking at one of the leaflets I had found in the boys' bathroom. It was an invitation to join in the desecration of Jewish graves this weekend in Vienna's Central Cemetery. There were pictures of a past incident with broken gravestones and jubilant skinheads dancing on the old graves.

"Why'd you keep this thing, Con?" she asked, handing it back and wiping her hands as if they were dirty.

"Curious, mostly. It's not that big a deal—not like they're really dangerous. A few old Nazis push over some gravestones and feel tough. Ignore it. I've lived in Austria my whole life, and nobody's ever made me feel discriminated against. Don't exaggerate this."

Her body stiffened.

Oops. Now I've really made her mad. Hannah wears her dark hair long. It falls down past her shoulders in thick, loose curls, and she never fusses with it like most girls. But when she's angry, she has a way of flipping it back with a toss of her head that says, "Get out of my way." The head went back now, and her dark eyes flashed with signals meant to make me feel like a very low life-form.

It worked, but I carefully hid it with an I-am-not-concerned slouch, wishing I had never picked up the stupid leaflet.

"Don't be so dumb, Con," she said with that sarcasm only girls can do. "Even you can't be that unconscious. Have you ever looked in the mirror? Blond hair, blue eyes—you look exactly like an Austrian and sound exactly like one, too. Not even an accent. What's to discriminate against?"

Thinking she might have a point, I didn't respond.

She continued to speak, less angry now but with a different edge to her voice that made me even more uncomfortable. "I've only lived here one year. But I've felt it. The looks, the remarks in German I can't understand whispered in the market . . . It's hard to explain, but don't tell me it isn't here. And it doesn't have to be pushing over old gravestones to hurt."

"You never said anything before," I responded, genuinely surprised. "But suppose it's true and people here still don't like Jews. How would they know you're Jewish?"

She pulled her white Skechers up onto the seat and her navy blue New York Giants sweat shirt down over her Levi's and looked at me like I was crazy.

"Con, I don't know if it's boys in general or just you in particular, but you can be sorta dense. With a last name like Goldberg, it isn't too hard to figure. And I don't exactly look like the Aryan heroine in some German myth or that stupid opera by Wagner we had to listen to in music class. I look Jewish. I'm glad I look Jewish. I'm not ashamed to look Jewish. But I do look Jewish."

Unsure how to answer that outburst, I was relieved when she moved on to a safer subject.

"And besides that, the idiots don't know much about graffiti. In New York, graffiti is an art form."

Totally relieved to be back on comfortable ground, I said, "Sure. Because you're from New York you're an expert on graffiti now? Along with everything else."

The driver ground through several gears as he attempted to slow down the heavy vehicle on the steep, winding hillside.

"Way to ruin a gearbox," I groaned, thinking about the contrast of riding home in this compared to a Mercedes limo.

"But who could have done it?" I went back to my original question. "It must have been a student; security's too tight for an outsider."

"Maybe. But probably not someone in your gifted, talented, and only-for-highly-intelligent-type-kids class," Hannah said sarcastically.

The school, and my mom, had forced me into some advanced classes because I made the mistake of doing well on the entrance exams last year. Everyone seemed to regret it, as my grades hadn't matched their expectations.

"And how did a non-gifted person like you come to that brilliant conclusion?" I asked.

"Because, Mr. Gifted and Talented, they misspelled foreigner: f-o-r-*i*-*e*-g-n-e-r-s."

We laughed. It was Hannah, not I, who had noticed the spelling error. So much for gifted and talented.

"What's the big deal over a little graffiti? And besides, whoever did it did us a favor," I said. The seriousness of the whole thing was wearing off already. "Who's going to remember a food fight after big stuff like that?"

I thought for a moment she was going to get angry again,

but it passed and she responded lightly.

"Good point." She relaxed for the first time since the assembly. "We were lucky today, Con. I still can't believe it worked so cool."

Even though no one sat close enough to overhear us, we lowered our voices—just in case—as we enjoyed remembering our afternoon triumph.

"Were we good or what?" she snickered.

During World History our stuffy teacher, Ms. Gaul, had sent us to her office to wait for yet another lecture on our performance and behavior in her class. Ms. Gaul's thin brown hair was always pulled back so tight it made her look like a face-lift in progress. She had an equally strained personality. Our efforts at brightening her life with a little humor had failed, and so we were banished to her office.

Expecting the standard lecture from her, we were busy thinking up excuses when Principal Miller stuck his head in and asked us to wait a little longer, as Ms. Gaul was going to be detained for about a half hour with an "emergency" in his office.

"I'm sure you have some studying to do while you wait," he had said naïvely.

"No problem," we assured him. Then we set about looking for any files on us or other interesting things we should know about.

Coming up empty and left with nothing better to do, Hannah sat down to try out Gaul's new IBM ThinkPad laptop computer. Hannah thinks she's an expert because her dad works for IBM.

I got this creative urge while I watched her type. Things come to me like that.

"Hannah," I said, raising my voice to a Ms. Gaul pitch and squinting my eyes like she does. "Hannah, take a memo to the students for me."

"Yes, ma'am," Hannah said in a most obsequious voice.

"What good news do you have for the kids today?"

"Well," I said, thinking quickly, watching the door for the teacher's arrival, "here it is: 'Notice to all AIS students! Food fights will be allowed only on the second Wednesday of every month and are to last no longer than ten minutes. Ms. Alberta Gaul.'"

Hannah laughed so hard I was sure someone was going to hear us, but she managed to print it and sign Gaul's name.

Ms. Gaul never made it out of her "emergency," and we went on to our next class via the lunchroom, where we tacked the note to the bulletin board. We figured no one read that stuff anyway.

The U.S. ambassador to Austria, the very honorable Herbert T. McCoy, happened to have a son in our class. Poor Tony. I'd long had a feeling he would like to break out of his ambassador's-son image—which so impressed the school officials, especially our prim princess of World History, the Gaul. Of all the important parents, Tony's dad was the most important.

Well, today Hannah and I had done a very good thing. We had helped Tony with a little self-expression. Although fate did play a part, it couldn't have happened without us.

We had positioned ourselves where we could see the notice board and watch for reactions. Tony was the first person to stop and actually read our memo. He walked in alone, paused, and read and reread our notice. A smile crossed his handsome face. He looked at us, but we gave away nothing. He knew, though. And we knew he knew. What happened next, even I could not have dreamed up. It was too perfect.

Tony sat down across from Leroy. Little Lord Leroy to us, he was the perfect teacher-pleaser. What a victim. We held our breath. Tony calmly ate most of his pizza, looked at his watch occasionally, and when it was nearly time for the bell, he did it. He threw a piece of very sloppy pizza right onto Leroy's neat white polo shirt. Pieces of mushrooms and pepperoni stuck in the red ooze. Tony then rather carefully wiped his hands and leaned back in his chair, waiting.

Silence. Total disbelief on Leroy's part finally gave way to high-pitched shrieking.

"You . . . you . . . creep. You little son of an ambassador . . . Spoiled little barbarian creep."

Quick intervention by the lunchroom supervisor prevented bloodshed, and when she demanded to know why Tony had done such a thing, he didn't even claim diplomatic immunity but very politely showed her the note on the bulletin board.

"See right here," he said. "Authorization for a food fight. This is the second Wednesday of October, and it certainly didn't last ten minutes."

Ms. Gaul had joined the show by that time, her face full of dismay that her prize—the ambassador's son—had fallen. He carefully explained to her, that yes, he thought it was "perfectly reasonable and consistent with her character to allow students some freedom of expression once a month."

Hannah and I left the lunchroom before we heard Ms. Gaul's response. However, when class resumed she had clearly recovered her composure and looked murderously at me. No one ever suspected Hannah, who took on a studious, innocent look perfectly. According to Ms. Gaul, Hannah was a wonderful student who occasionally fell under my bad influence. Ha! Looks could be very misleading.

We were nearly to my street by the time we had relived the whole wonderful episode. I decided it was time to tell Hannah about my next plan. No more following strangers on trams hoping for excitement—this was the real thing. There was a spy or spies around, Branko had said. And the more I thought about it, the more I thought it might be him. He was probably passing secrets for other Croatians, in their continuing bitter struggle against the Serbians, through his innocent-looking bakery. If Hannah and I could prove what Branko was doing, he would have to let us help. And we could carry information for him or pass stuff to his people. Who would suspect a couple of kids?

At first Hannah was uncertain of my sanity as I told her my suspicions of Branko and my plan to uncover his spying activity—or some other spy person I hadn't thought of yet. But she finally agreed that my sanity had never been that certain anyway and it sounded like fun. She didn't actually admit it, but I could tell Hannah thought it was a great idea, and we agreed to meet at Gregor's house that evening to organize our strategy.

"We need a place to work where no one will ask questions. Like a 'safe house.' And his place is perfect," I assured her. "Gregor's parents let him do anything. They wouldn't even notice a spy ring being run from his room."

She rolled her eyes at me, muttering something about reading too many spy novels, but in the end we agreed.

"Can you meet me there at seven-thirty this evening?" I asked, jumping up as I heard the bus driver call my stop.

"It's number 75-A. Up Braungasse two blocks, 75-A." I shouted Gregor's house number through the window as the bus pulled off, hoping she had heard me. Only as the creaky old bus moved away did I notice I was waving at her with the Nazi leaflet still clutched in my hand.

4

FORGETTING TO REMEMBER

WARM APPLE STRUDEL GREETED US AS GREGOR'S MOTHER ushered Hannah and me into her scrupulously clean kitchen. She invited us to sit and have some of the delicious pastry while we waited for Gregor to return with his dad.

"I'm sorry Gregor is not here," she apologized, hovering over us and nervously brushing up any crumbs that skipped off our plates.

"Is this place always this neat?" Hannah whispered when Frau Müller left the room for a minute.

I kept eating—trying to contain my crumbs as the flaky pastry broke away when I cut it with my fork. I didn't dare pick it up and eat it with my fingers in case fussy Frau Müller came back in.

Hannah looked nervously at the door of the kitchen for her return. "I wish she would stop hovering. She looks at me funny, Con. Did you notice that? And she could hardly shake my hand when you introduced me."

"Oh brother, Hannah, you're imagining things again. Relax and eat the Strudel." I shrugged. "She may be a little weird, but she sure can cook."

"You worry about your stomach a lot, Con," Hannah replied. But she took another piece, and we went on eating until a large portion of the plate of Austria's famous delicacy was gone.

I had prepared a list of people to investigate and a plan to go about checking them out. Eager to show Hannah, I decided to wait until we were safely in Gregor's room. I wished he would hurry up and return.

"By the way," Hannah asked me, "what was in that note from Ms. Gaul you were so worried about yesterday?"

"You'll love this," I laughed. "All that sweat and it wasn't even about me. It was a special invitation for Mom to join PTA again this year . . . and run for president." I shook my head thinking about all that wasted worry.

"Ha. Serves you right for having such a guilty conscience. Is she going to do it?"

"Not a chance. She went to PTA last year and hated the end-less meetings and vowed never to go again. 'I will climb the highest mountain or swim the deepest sea for you, Con, but I refuse to go to PTA ever again.' "

"I like your mom," Hannah said. "She's not real normal."

"You can say that again."

Frau Müller flitted back in again, still apologizing, explaining that Herr Müller had taken Gregor out to buy a video game he had been begging for.

Desperate for a topic of conversation, I made the mistake of telling her about the neo-Nazi vandalism at school.

Frau Müller was a slightly pudgy, overly neat woman who always looked like she was going out, even when cleaning her already tidy house. Tight little curls framed her round, rosy face, which took on a distinctly dark look as I blundered on about the leaflet, the swastikas, the threats from the principal to find and punish the guilty parties, and his announcement that all students and staff would be required to attend a Holocaust lecture next week.

I related it with a matter-of-fact voice and didn't notice Hannah's growing discomfort as she watched Frau Müller.

"Humph. That's nonsense," Frau Müller said, nervously wiping away at imaginary crumbs. "Holocaust. Remember the

Holocaust. We are sick of foreigners who don't understand telling us to remember. I think we should be allowed to forget the past."

She was looking at me, talking only to me, as though Hannah weren't there. But it was Hannah who responded, and while her German might not have been perfect, her meaning was clear.

"I think it's obvious people have already done a good job of forgetting, Frau Müller."

At that moment Herr Müller and Gregor came bursting in, and we escaped from the tense situation and oppressive neatness of Frau Müller's kitchen up to Gregor's room and the business of the evening.

◆

"What's up?" Gregor asked. "What's so secret that you can't tell me over the phone?"

We settled down in his large room on the fourth floor of their apartment building. There were two tall windows facing the street at treetop level. It was dark outside and, unlike yesterday, warm and still. The trees were unmoving. Gregor had built-in bookshelves and a desk along one wall. It was as messy as his mom's kitchen was neat. School books were strewn among comic books, dozens of computer and video games, and a half-eaten banana. A poster of Darrell Green of the Washington Redskins, which I had given him, covered a portion of one wall. Hannah sat leaning against Green's knees in a desk chair covered with soft leather cushions. Gregor and I sprawled on top of the eiderdown comforter that covered his bed.

"What'd he say?" asked Hannah. "Don't talk so fast, Gregor."

"I wish you'd work on your German so we could move a little faster," I told her, but I proceeded to translate where necessary and told them both my plan.

I took my list of the most likely suspects out of my pocket

and laid it out for them to see, warning them not to reveal any of this to any adults. All adults were suspects until proven otherwise.

Gregor looked skeptical and said, "Even our parents?"

"Sure—why not?" Hannah put in. "Being parents could be great cover."

"Well, I can tell you right now, my mother is not spy material," Gregor exclaimed.

I certainly agreed but didn't tell him so.

My list had three categories: Practically Impossible, Not Likely, and Suspicious.

Branko Loveric was at the top under the Suspicious category. The other names were listed in no special order or category. Comprised of the people I knew best in Vienna, it included Austrians, Americans, and other foreigners living in Austria.

The list read:

Dr. Reiks
Frau Reiks
Herr von Hofmannsthal
Frau Schnively
Nigel Kaye
Roberta Kaye
Aaron Goldberg
Ruth Goldberg
Herr Müller
Frau Müller
Rev. Randy Martin
Alice Martin

On the back of the page, I had listed different traits for analysis: Physical Characteristics, Behavior Patterns, Possible Motives, Qualifications, and Opportunity.

I had already penciled in PI for Practically Impossible by some names, including the Müllers'. Hannah and I had agreed that our mothers were totally incapable of leading two lives. They had enough trouble with one. Also, we knew them too well, there was no motive, and definitely no opportunity. They were always around making sure that we were around.

My mom did go out to the university on Mondays and Thursdays. But since it was for a Hebrew class, it didn't count.

"Who is von Hofmannsthal?" Hannah asked.

"He's a famous opera singer," Gregor explained, obviously surprised Hannah had never heard of him.

"And Herr von Hofmannsthal is our dear landlady's favorite tenant," I said. "He's an idiot, no doubt—how else could you go around performing Wagner's month-long operas? But he does travel all over Europe, and he has a real cushy life for someone who makes a living singing opera."

"It's possible, I guess," Gregor said, and we listed him as NL for Not Likely—but possible.

"Your mom is always traveling to London or Washington, D.C., without you, Con. That is suspicious, no?" Gregor asked.

"Hardly," I answered. "She does research for her writing. What information would she pass on anyway—how bad my grades are? I don't think so. Only my grandparents would be interested, and even they wouldn't pay for that information. No way. Not my mom."

Hannah and I agreed it couldn't be our moms, but we decided to at least consider our dads.

"Who's Rev. Randy Martin?" Hannah and Gregor both wanted to know.

"He's the pastor of our English-speaking church. And they are very good friends of ours. Mom knew them in the States."

"Preachers aren't spies," Hannah said.

"At first I thought so, too," I explained. "But just think about it. He has opportunity and contacts in the church. Lots of diplomats and business people from all over the world attend. They could even slip secrets to him in the offering plate. Who'd suspect that?"

"No one!" they said together, Hannah in English, Gregor in German.

"Absolutely no one but you," Hannah added, laughing at me.

"See, it's perfect," I said. "And besides, his wife, Alice, takes people on tours to the Middle East every summer. They both have possible motive—they are loyal Americans. Qualifications—both speak English and German, and in her case add French. Opportunities—unlimited."

I put an S by each of their names for Suspicious.

After some discussion about Frau Schnively, we crossed her off and moved on to our family doctor, Dr. Reiks, and his wife, who is a nurse. They have been good friends, and we have even joined them at their old village near the Hungarian border for a weekend in the country. I wondered about him because he loved to tell me stories about World War II and hiding out from the Russians. When we visited their country home, he showed me something very odd. In a cellar under the house, he had hundreds of jars of honey. Row upon row, most of it brown and solid—but honey is always good, he assured me. It is so pure it can never spoil.

Dr. Reiks' family nearly starved when the Russian soldiers killed and ate their animals, destroyed the garden, and took all the food in their farmhouse. They lived on honey from their beehives; that's why he continued to store it. Just in case. It was clear to me he still hated the Russians, but it was less clear whom he would work for or why now that the Cold War was over. Neither of the Reikses spoke anything but German, and they were very busy taking care of his patients. We put NL by both their names.

"I don't think IBM would allow spying by their employees," Hannah said as we moved down the list. "That leaves out my dad. But Nigel is a very interesting possibility."

"Why?" I asked, thinking he was the least likely person for such undercover work.

"Well, for one thing he's British. James Bond is British; it's a tradition with them. And you don't know much about him yet. Who knows what kind of background he might have?"

"Nigel is not James Bond." I laughed. "Mom would kill him. No, he's not the type."

Then I told them my theory about Branko, leaving out the part about judo, since I promised. But I filled them in on the skinhead waiting outside the bakery for a man leaving with no bakery goods. I got sidetracked telling Gregor about the Jaguar, but Hannah brought us back with her sometimes annoyingly practical perspective.

"Maybe they were out of the bread he wanted. Did you ever think about that, Con? People do go in shops and come out empty-handed."

I don't think either Hannah or Gregor was impressed by my brush with death, but in the end they agreed that Branko at least had motive with the current unrest in his homeland. The bakery could be a front.

"I need to go home now," Hannah said, heading for the door. "Sorry I can't stay and see your new video game, Gregor, but I'll alert our best agents by phone when I get home and tell them to start surveillance of Branko and the Martins," she added dryly.

"Very funny, Hannah. We'll check them out ourselves," Gregor said. "How about meeting Saturday morning to discuss how?"

"Can't," I replied. "We're going to Grossgmain this weekend. I'll call you both when we get back on Sunday evening. Hannah and I have a lot of experience following people. We'll teach you, Gregor—right, Hannah?"

She nodded in agreement as she opened the door rather suddenly and smacked Frau Müller right in the face.

"Sorry," Hannah panicked. "I didn't mean to. I'm so sorry, Frau Müller."

Gregor and I leaped up to see if Frau Müller was hurt, which seemed not to be the case as she managed a weak smile, mumbled something about passing at the wrong moment, and continued down the hall past Gregor's room to her own.

We all looked at each other. Could she have been listening? Why would she be listening?

After Hannah left, Gregor and I stopped worrying about his mother and went downstairs to his father's study.

High-tech mayhem from his Soundblaster greeted us as Gregor booted up the new game his dad had loaded on the computer while we had been planning our spy search.

"What kind of game is this, Gregor?" A large red swastika on a black background covered the screen. Chimneys slowly appeared in the background. Smoke curled up from the chimneys forming two words: *KL MANAGER*.

"Fighting Nazis, is it?" I was getting excited at the prospect of playing a new game. Gregor flexed his fingers eagerly over the keyboard, excitement pouring out of his somewhat overweight frame.

He gently tapped the keys without depressing them as the intro rolled past. Vibrating sounds from the blaster were building as the option screen revealed the choices to begin. Gregor placed the cursor on *CAMP 1* and clicked the mouse. An aerial view of a military-looking compound came up. It included a railroad, barracks, and hospital, with barbed wire surrounding the whole area.

Before I could read what all the different buildings were, Gregor placed the cursor on the hospital and clicked the mouse. We were in a corridor now, each side lined with five or six doors, a different German word on every door. Gregor used the arrow keys to maneuver into the first room on the right. The sign on the door said *WHIP*. Click. Now we were inside a room.

A sinister-looking man in a military uniform, with a cigarette dangling from the corner of his mouth, stood in a gray room with a picture of Hitler in the background. He was clutching a whip. Behind him was a nearly naked man with dark hair and a hooked nose, hanging by his hands. Gregor pushed F1 and then Enter. The whip cracked, and the man screamed as blood poured out.

"Gregor, that's gross," I said, horrified. "What's the purpose of this game?"

"To win, of course, like all games. To kill Jews. Look, you can switch weapons." He used the arrow key again and we were in a similar room, but the man held a police baton. *Thud. Thud.* The blows came down on the hanging man.

Gregor was so absorbed with moving on to the next victim, the next weapon, that he didn't sense my uneasiness. I asked again, "What is this about?"

For an answer, he placed the cursor on the picture of Hitler in the back of the room and enhanced the detail level. Words over the swastika became clear on the screen: *AUSCHWITZ.*

"That's sick," I said. "It's a concentration camp game. These things are illegal."

Ignoring me, he tapped Enter two times and the beatings continued.

"Gregor, at least turn the sound off. Your parents are going to hear," I said nervously.

He stopped then, the figures on the screen also stopping in midtorture, raised his hands off the keyboard, and looked at me with disgust.

"My dad loaded it, dummy. He plays it, too. Why are you so uptight about a game? Besides, you fight Nazis in your games. Killing Nazis, killing Jews—what's the difference? That's what my dad says. If you don't like it, don't play. Or leave."

I didn't play, but I didn't leave, either, not for a while. Walking home along the quiet street, listening to the dry leaves crackle under my feet, I wondered how Gregor could play that game. I was glad Hannah had left early. But before I reached my gate, I began to feel better. If his parents let him play and even played with him, it couldn't be that bad.

And Gregor didn't need to worry. I wasn't about to tell anyone, especially my mom or Hannah. Neither one of them would understand that it was only a game.

THE SANDS OF TIME

"O-O-O-O-OH YE-AHH. . . !" SO CONCLUDED MY BEATLES medley serenade to Frau Schnively Friday morning, sung at the top of my voice in the shower.

We were going to Grossgmain at noon, and I was going to miss World History and dear old Ms. Gaul. Either one of those things would have been enough to make me sing without the added incentive of the reaction upstairs. Frau Schnively was easily irritated, especially when my singing floated up to her apartment so early in the morning.

Midway through my performance, Nigel stuck his head in the bathroom door.

"Con, I say, Con," he shouted at me, "can you whistle?"

"Sure," I said, ready to give him a sample.

"Good," he replied, shutting the door, "because you certainly can't sing."

Nigel still looked pleased with himself when I joined him in the kitchen for breakfast, which was usually "help yourself to an English muffin" in our house.

"Very funny," I said. "Is that what passes for humor in Great Britain?"

He just laughed quietly and went on reading the morning paper. Nigel was tall, six foot four at least, and on the thin side. He looked dignified in his dark business suits. And although not nearly as stuffy as he looked (nobody who drove like Nigel could be stuffy), I still felt it was my duty to loosen him up a little.

"Here, Nigel—read this." I handed him a copy of the Abbott and Costello routine Hannah and I had done in drama class last week. "You be Costello," I said.

A: Now, on the St. Louis team we have Who's on first, What's on second. I Don't Know is on third.
C: That's what I want to find out.
A: I'm telling you. Who's on first, What's on second, I Don't Know is on third.
C: Well, all I'm trying to find out is what's the guy's name on first base.
A: Oh, no, no. What's on second base.
C: I'm not asking you who's on second.
A: Who's on first.
C: That's what I'm trying to find out.
A: Well, don't change the players around.
C: I'm not changing nobody.
A: Now, take it easy.
C: What's the guy's name on first base?
A: What's the guy's name on second base.
C: I'm not askin' ya who's on second.
A: Who's on first.
C: I don't know.
A: Please. Now, what is it you want to know?
C: What is the fellow's name on third base?
A: What is the fellow's name on second base.
C: I'm not askin' ya who's on second.
A: Who's on first.
C: I don't know.

Mom walked in as we both broke up laughing.

"Con, are you doing that goofy routine again? I thought you and Hannah were never going to get through it one time without collapsing into giggles. It isn't that funny."

"Women," I said.

She walked over and gave Nigel a hug. "You were kinda cute doing Costello with your accent, though."

He looked as though she had just called him the king of England.

"Okay, you two," Nigel said. "This is enough happiness for one morning. Somebody has to work in this family. Be at my office to pick me up at one, and we can make it to Grossgmain in time for tea."

Nigel grabbed his briefcase and added, "I have to run or I'll miss the number 48. Take care of my car."

Mom followed him out, and I sat daydreaming of her fainting on our way to Nigel's office. Taking over the wheel, I would brilliantly maneuver the BMW through traffic, arriving at the hospital in time for Mom to be revived. I would be a hero and recognized as the probable Grand Prix race-driving champion of the future.

———————————— ◆ ————————————

It didn't work out exactly like that. In fact, we had an uneventful drive through the city from my school in the Vienna Woods to the banks of the Danube River and Nigel's office building.

The day was warm for mid-October, the sunroof open and the windows down. I pulled off my Redskins baseball cap and let the sun warm my face as I gloated over missing an afternoon of school, leaving Vienna behind, and seeing my old friends in Grossgmain and hiking in the nearby Untersberg Mountains.

Mom and I had lived in Grossgmain for the first thirteen years of my life. Nine kilometers west of Salzburg, Grossgmain sits at the foot of the Alps, with houses dotted around it like dozens of other Austrian villages.

I loved the mountains behind our apartment. Deep woods with deer and small game led up to castle ruins where I used to play with my friends. There are big farmhouses hidden away in the woods that look like pictures in my *Grimm's Fairy Tales* and are probably as old as those stories. I especially loved to hunt rabbit in the forest with my friend Herr Donner.

"Whatever made us move to Grossgmain in the first place, Mom?" I don't know what made me ask that, but lately things I had always taken for granted seemed . . . well, unusual. I looked at her. "I mean the *real* reason."

"Real reason?" she replied.

"Yeah. Reasons that I was too young to understand before."

"Before what?" Mom kidded me. "Before you became an adult at age fifteen?"

"Mom . . . I'm serious. You had no family there. It would have been easier in the States—wouldn't it? I mean, there are universities where you could have studied at home. Why Austria?" I insisted.

Distracted by a tram turning through our lane—or perhaps just trying to avoid answering me—Mom concentrated on driving.

Every summer we had gone to the States. And each time the family had tried to convince Mom not to return to Europe. Especially my father's brothers and sisters and his parents, Grandpa and Grandma Rea. But just as regularly she had said, "One more year . . . then we'll see," and I wondered if we would ever move to the United States—especially now that Mom had married an Englishman.

For the thousandth time I wished my life were as simple as my cousins' in the States.

"Why?" Mom finally answered kiddingly. "The *why* would probably take Freud to figure out. . . . Maybe I need a visit to his couch, too."

We had just passed number 19 Berggasse, where Sigmund Freud had lived and worked. Mom was referring to the time my class had visited Freud's home, which is now a museum. The curator, a terribly boring little man, had left the room to take a phone call. Unfortunately it was a short call, and he returned to find me trying out the famous couch and my classmate Ted Berkins psychoanalyzing me. The curator was not amused.

And now Mom was hedging.

"Mom!" I prodded. "Forget my childish pranks and answer the question."

"Okay, Con—but there isn't any deep secret. You know the facts. I'm sorry I can't satisfy your vivid imagination with a good story. I was visiting my old college roommate who lived in Germany at the time. You were just a tiny baby, your father had died only a few months earlier, and I needed some distance from memories and too much family. So when we visited Salzburg, I checked out the university and found I could finish my German studies there. It seemed . . . well, logical."

Mom paused, a faraway expression on her face as if she were remembering that time and had forgotten I was there. "Donner," she said almost to herself. "Herr Donner had a 'Zimmer frei,' which we rented for the night in Grossgmain because all the hotels in Salzburg were booked solid. And that . . . that was the beginning."

"Beginning of what?" I asked, tension rising in me from the way she even said our old landlord's name.

Mom looked slightly startled. "Of living there, of course. We moved into his attic apartment shortly after that. You know the rest."

I leaned back in the seat and watched a jet fly across my line of sight, then out of it toward the airport.

"There must have been more to it than that," I insisted.

"Grossgmain was a lovely, quiet village close to the city. I could study, the Donners were very friendly, and they offered to help look out for you while I went to school. You took to one another instantly. And that was that." She said this with some degree of finality.

There was more to it than that, I felt sure. But I didn't want to spoil the day with too many questions, certainly not on the sore subject of our not very friendly move out of the Donners' apartment building. I couldn't understand Mom's unreasonable attitude about a man who had been our friend for as long as I could remember. Anyway, just then we pulled up at number 5 Handelskai, Nigel's office.

He was ready and waiting.

"Glad to see you arrived on time and in one piece," Nigel said, grinning. "Let me put my briefcase in the boot and check for scratches; then we'll be on our way."

Mom made a face at him as he folded himself into the driver's seat. "What did you expect?" she asked.

"Don't answer that, Nigel," I advised him as I got comfortable in the backseat. "This is one trip I'm looking forward to. It won't take as long as usual, eh, Mom?"

"Um . . . probably not. Riding in the Fiat is something of a Third World experience in terms of comfort and speed," she said.

"You can say that again. Mercedes used to shudder in horror as they passed us on the Autobahn." I sighed with pleasure. "They'll have trouble catching us today, right, Nigel?"

"Never even smell us," he said, deftly avoiding an oncoming tram. Their tracks wandered all over the city streets. It was a driver's job to avoid the trams, not the other way around. Mom managed that most of the time. But I knew there were a few tram drivers out there with memories of near-misses on their minds and evil desire in their hearts should they ever again see that old blue Fiat with international tags.

Traffic slowed us down to a crawl past Schönbrunn Palace. It was always like that here with swarms of tourists coming to see the old Hapsburg palace where Marie Antoinette grew up before becoming France's queen.

Finally the road opened up and we left the suburbs of Vienna behind. Entering the west Autobahn, we headed toward Salzburg at a more enjoyable speed.

"The air in Grossgmain is clean, the view is magnificent, and best of all, it's quiet." Mom looked at Nigel. "I am so glad we're finally going to see it together."

"Personally, I hate the quiet. Did you know they actually have quiet laws?" I asked Nigel.

"What, may I ask, are quiet laws?" Nigel finally tore his eyes off Mom and woke up to my remark. Nigel was, above all, polite.

"A pain," I said. "I once told my cousins in the States about the midday quiet curfew. They laughed so hard I pretended to have made the whole thing up."

"Constantine," my mother said in mock horror.

"It would be unconstitutional in America to keep everyone quiet for two hours a day so some old dearies could get their rest. It was a pain!"

"Only for small boys and dogs. The rest of us liked it. Many people in Grossgmain are wealthy retirees from Germany," she told Nigel. "They come for mountain air, peace and quiet, and they bring piles of Deutsch Mark, so the Bürgermeister makes sure they get exactly what they want in his little village."

"Sounds civilized to me," Nigel said, "after the month I've had." He looked at Mom. "It won't always be so hectic, Roberta. I promise."

Mom looked slightly embarrassed at his apology and shifted the conversation. "When is your next trip to Russia? I'd like you to pick up a couple of things for me. Some presents for my nieces out in Oregon and Wyoming."

He groaned. "Only for you would I go into one of those tourist traps. I used to laugh at other men carrying home bags from those places."

"Ha. It will do you good," Mom said.

"Anyway, I don't have to go for about a month. Thank goodness. I should get hazardous pay to fly Aeroflot."

"What's wrong with Aeroflot?" I asked as we crossed over the Danube curving its way back to Vienna.

"Most things," Nigel replied firmly. "It's a disaster of an

airline. The food and service could kill you even if you're lucky enough not to crash. Private enterprise hasn't yet reached Aeroflot."

"Fly the frightening skies, huh?"

"Dead right," Nigel said with a smile.

We were cruising. No speed limits on the Autobahn, so it was a surprise when a red Jaguar went sailing past. He must have been doing 170 kilometers at least.

"Nigel!" I screamed. "That's him! Catch up with that car. Come on, hurry up. That's the same guy who tried to run me over."

"Con, you're crazy. We aren't going to try to catch that car. This isn't a movie." Mom turned around and looked at me as if I had lost my mind. "Don't you think it's possible there are two red Jaguars in Austria?"

But Nigel had in fact put his foot down a little, and I could feel the BMW surge forward.

"What makes you think it's the same car, Con? There are lots of red Jags around." Nigel had taken the story about my near-miss more seriously than anyone else. "Did you see the driver when he went around just now?"

"No," I admitted. "I didn't see him. But there aren't many E-types, and if we get close, I could tell you for sure if it's the same skinhead."

The Autobahn was open and flat, and the car steadily pulled away from us.

"Come on," I urged Nigel. "We can do it."

"Maybe," he said. "I wouldn't mind having a look, but that's a hot car and we don't want to push it."

He said that last bit looking at Mom, who let out a sigh of relief.

"We're losing him," I moaned. I could barely see him now.

"If he stays on the Autobahn, we will catch him, Con. There's a spot coming up by Mondsee where he will have to slow. You watch the service spots to see if he pulls off. And we'll have a look. I'll stay with him."

Mom mumbled something about Nigel humoring me.

I spent the next hour watching. Sometimes we had him in sight. Nigel kept his word—he was pushing it, even for him.

We flew around a curve and dropped sharply down to Mondsee, a typical Austrian village with a beautiful lake surrounding it. We had dropped out of the sunshine and into the gloom of fairly thick fog. The clouds hung low over the water, covering most of the lake and the town from view. But better than sunshine was the bright red car pulling out in front of us.

"There he is! There he is!" I yelled. But Nigel saw him first and pulled up beside him, trapping the car in the right lane behind a slower car.

"That's him," I shouted. But it wasn't. No skinhead. No angry, ugly face. Just an irritated rich guy wanting Nigel to move so he could get past.

"Are you sure?" Nigel asked. "He doesn't look much like your description."

"Nigel, we've seen enough. Let him pass," Mom said nervously as the guy began to make vulgar gestures at Nigel and edge his car closer.

"Afraid not," I said disappointed. "It isn't even a '72 model."

As I said that, Nigel let off the gas and allowed the angry man to pass.

"Con, your imagination does tend to carry you away," Mom chided. "You need to begin to live in the real world—where you do your homework, not look for spies."

Nigel closed the sunroof since the sun was gone, and we drove the next several kilometers much more slowly in the fog. I knew Mom wouldn't understand, so I didn't bother to explain. That wasn't the same guy, but I hadn't imagined what had happened at the bakery. The men in the Jaguar had not been normal customers, and Branko had acted strangely about the whole thing. Very strangely.

Finally Mom broke the silence. "I do hope these clouds lift. You must see Grossgmain in the sunshine to fully appreciate it."

"Don't worry," Nigel said. "We still have about thirty kilometers to go. Maybe it will be nice there. Anyway, I'm looking forward to dinner in that wonderful restaurant you two have been raving about, the Vortel. There's nothing like a big plate of French fries to lift the spirits, eh, Con? Especially when nestled right next to a giant Schnitzel."

"True. They don't beat theirs to death, either."

"What does that mean?" Nigel asked.

"Nothing," Mom said, smiling at me. "Nothing at all."

The fog was still thick as pea soup when we drove into Grossgmain. But Nigel was right—after two Cokes, a plate of French fries, and a Schnitzel, the gloom had definitely lifted. At least inside.

The Vortel was actually a hotel as well as a restaurant, and it had been there when Christopher Columbus discovered America. The same family had been running it ever since, for over five hundred years!

The German border was only fifty yards down the road that ran in front of the Vortel. The road led directly to Berchtesgaden, which was the mountain town where Hitler and his cohorts had their vacation homes. The Vortel dining room was a favorite stop of theirs on their way up the mountain.

Göring, Bormann, Hess, Speer, and Hitler—they all ate here and probably left signed pictures for the walls. None of the pictures would be up now, of course, and the management did not like to brag about its past, at least not to Americans. But there were those who had lived here in Hitler's day, and they would quietly talk. Sometimes. Mom had a way of turning conversations in that direction, I had explained to Nigel when recounting all the local history for him while we waited for our food.

Many people in Grossgmain still remembered us. Especially the ones in the Vortel—our dining room away from home when we lived around the corner on Poststrasse.

Looking around the place, I couldn't see that much had changed. Most of the people were wearing the traditional Bavarian dress. The women in Dirndln and the men in Lederhosen, their plumed hats hanging from wooden pegs on the walls.

Underneath many of the tables, long-haired dachshunds slept while their owners overate.

"Meine güte! The little Constantine." Our waitress gushed as she recognized us. She leaned over, about to pinch my cheeks, but must have thought better of it when she saw the look I gave her.

"How you have grown!" She went on and on. "Meine güte, look how he has grown up."

How amazingly clever of me, I thought to myself.

Others stopped by, too. The men shook Nigel's hand warmly, and the women tut-tutted excitedly when Mom introduced him as her husband.

Mom and Nigel ordered coffee, and just when I wondered if any of my old school friends might show up before we left, in came Herr and Frau Donner. In Bavarian dress like nearly everyone else, they looked typically Austrian but stood out at once. He was bigger than anyone in the village and had this loud, booming voice that filled up the room when he walked in. Tonight was no exception. He didn't see me at first as I waved to them, surrounded as he was by several men greeting him at the door.

"Over here," I shouted in spite of Mom's obvious disapproval. I pointed to a spot next to us.

"Constantine! My little friend," he bellowed. Rushing ahead of his poor wife, as usual, he shook my hand with so much vigor it ended up a bear hug. "You are early. I didn't expect you until tomorrow." He turned to Mom and Nigel, and introductions were made all around.

We made room at our table, and the small talk was friendly

enough. I was glad to see them, especially Herr Donner. I hoped Nigel would like him.

I had been bugging Mom for months, so she finally called the Donners and made plans with them to visit our old apartment. It was vacant now, and I wanted to show it to Nigel.

"Please finish your coffee so we can go," I said, reaching for my jacket. It was hot and stuffy in the restaurant, and I felt as if I had eaten too many pieces of Sachertorte—a wonderful Austrian chocolate cake.

Mom made no move to go. Instead, she put another little spoon of whipped cream in what remained of her coffee, stirring it slowly and deliberately. There was a crack in her otherwise outwardly friendly manner when she coolly asked Herr Donner if he had ever found that hunting knife he was missing when we were last here.

My coat stopped in midair, half on, half off. Donner's smile changed to a scowl, and his laughter dried up. Nigel, too, must have known what she was referring to, because he breathed her name very quietly, questioningly.

Mom avoided my eyes and Nigel's protest. She just went on stirring her coffee, waiting for an answer.

Herr Donner's answer was muffled as he stood up, motioning his wife to join him. "No . . . I have not found the knife . . . and . . . Con's right, it is getting late. We'll see you in the morning." His exasperation with Mom was not far below the surface.

I stood there staring after them. I couldn't believe she had done that.

"What is it with you, Mom? Why did you have to do that?" I didn't even try to hide my emotions as I continued putting on my jacket.

"Where are you going, Con?" Her voice was sharp.

"Out. I want to walk through the woods. Alone! I'll meet you at the Pension."

"Wait, Con. I'm sorry," Mom said with a softer voice. "Please sit down."

I didn't sit, but I didn't walk out, either.

She tried to explain. "Watching Donner all evening, with everyone who stopped at our table to butter him up and say hello—the big man in the village—and your feelings for him so obvious—"

"What's wrong with my feelings?" I interrupted her. "Friendly feelings for an old man who has always been my friend. That's bad?" I was close to yelling.

"No. Of course not. And calm down. I just sort of . . . I don't know. . . . I wanted to remind you of how he treated Hannah, accusing her of stealing his hunting knife when we all knew she couldn't have, and the way he treated her all that day, for that matter. You noticed it, too, Con. Remember?"

I remembered. And remembering made me uncomfortable. I had begged and begged Mom, and she finally agreed to a picnic with the Donners last summer. We brought Hannah with us. The day was great, except . . . except for one thing. Even I had to admit Herr Donner seemed rude and unfriendly to Hannah that whole day. He had looked at her funny, as though he hated her, but that was impossible since he had never even met her before. I had pushed it out of my mind then, but it had been odd. I shook off the feeling as I remembered the looks he had given her.

But that hadn't been the worst of it. While Hannah and I hiked up to the Plainburg Ruins by ourselves, he accused her of stealing a valuable hunting knife during the picnic. Mom exploded at him but did not tell me about it until after we dropped off Hannah at home that evening.

On the way home Mom had done a good job of keeping up a front with friendly talk about the day and the beautiful mountains. But I watched her a little nervously and saw a very angry, brooding undercurrent. I never knew what Mom told Herr Donner. As usual Frau Donner stayed out of the confrontation, standing in the background, supportive but quiet. But it was a long time before either one of them called me again. I had hoped this weekend would make things better.

"I say, Con, I could use some air myself." Nigel stood up and quietly took charge. "Let's walk together, and your mom can bring the car around when she's ready."

He laid the keys on the table, his arm resting gently around my shoulders as we headed for the door.

It was still foggy when we got outside, and the old church next door was ringing its giant bell. We stood for a moment listening to that familiar sound, breathing in the fresh, cool air.

"Lead the way. This is your town," he said.

I knew Nigel was trying to cheer me up and make me forget what happened back in the restaurant. I knew and I appreciated it—and also how he had believed me and chased the Jaguar. Surprised he didn't always take Mom's side as I had expected, I wanted to thank him but couldn't think of how to say it.

"Why the bells now?" he asked. "It seems an odd time to ring them."

"Sometimes they ring to warn of a coming storm," I answered, looking up at the sky. "It used to warn the farmers to get out of the fields or get in their herds. Seems a little silly in this TV age, doesn't it?"

"Much friendlier than a TV and probably just as accurate," he said.

We walked briskly up Poststrasse past our old apartment. The house looked very much like all the others in town. It was an old chalet style with a slanting roof and window boxes filled with flowers. Natural wooden shutters framed each window.

We stopped to look at the dark house. I guessed the Donners had not gone directly home. We could make out the window of our old front room, a little attic window.

Why did Mom have to ruin this night? I thought, feeling angry again.

"Nice place, this town," Nigel said. "It looks quiet, safe, and beautiful. No wonder you lived here so long."

"Wait till you see it in the morning, with the mountains and everything. Sometimes we could even ski from our apartment to the slopes."

"Good heavens, man! No wonder you are better than I am," he said, referring to our one and only ski trip last winter when I had wiped him out. "That's not fair. I grew up in Africa and never saw a flake of snow till I came to Europe as an adult. You grew up with a ski slope out your front door."

"Sure, Nigel, go ahead and make excuses. Look, I can't help it. Some of us have it, some of us don't."

The tension broke, and I told him tales of Grossgmain as we walked toward the woods behind the Donners' house. I pointed out Frau Rozstoski's house, too, and shouted at her window, hoping she'd come out. "Must have her hearing aid off," I said. "You'll see her tomorrow."

"Where is our inn, anyway? Shouldn't we be there by now?" Nigel asked after we had come out of the woods and onto a street.

"Yup. There it is. 'Pension Eibel.' " A wooden sign in the shape of a hunter's horn stood by the road. The pension was hidden by trees. We walked in the loose gravel up the drive, making loud crunching noises. The BMW was nowhere to be seen, so we went in.

Nigel and I looked at all the hunting things hanging on the walls while we waited for Herr Eibel to finish with the registration form. There were wicked-looking traps, rifles, and stuffed animal heads of various sizes.

Behind the desk, over Herr Eibel's head, was a World War II Schmeisser. Several medals hung next to it with their swastikas missing from the circles underneath the spread eagle. The outlines of where they had been were clearly evident. Herr Eibel noticed my curiosity and moved in the way of my gaze. *Strange*, I thought. *Why put them up?* I felt his eyes on me as I moved away, still looking at all the things on his walls. I felt along the spot where the lightning symbol of the SS once had been sewn on a cap, also missing but with the faded shape clearly evident.

Herr Eibel reminded me more of a hunter than an inn-keeper. Pension Eibel had once been an inn mainly for hunters, and these mountains were still full of game, according to the locals. But the laws had changed and hunting was illegal now—except for rabbits. So the Pension had changed with the times, and now all that was left of those days hung on the walls and decorated the inn throughout. At least that was all we could see of its past. What else remained was a mystery. The memory of World War II was still there. Like so many places in beautiful little Grossgmain, as Mom said, it hovered out of sight but definitely not out of mind.

◆

Later, when Mom had joined us at the Pension Eibel, I went to bed with a new Asterix book while Mom and Nigel went downstairs to have a glass of hot mulled apple cider.

Half an hour later, after laughing my way through *Asterix and the Legionary*, I thought about how it bugged Mom that I still read the Asterix cartoon books. The fact that everybody in Europe—young and old—read them still escaped her.

Sometimes I couldn't figure out my mom. She was always telling me how we had to be honest with each other. Always wanting me to tell her my feelings. But more and more, I knew she was not being completely honest with me. How could she expect me to be honest if she wasn't?

As the damp air invaded my room from the partially opened window, the fluffy eiderdown felt good. I finally put down the book, turned out the light, and listened for the train.

When I had lived in Grossgmain, I liked to fall asleep waiting for the train to whistle. It always came. My good-night benediction, I had called it. Like the benediction at church when Rev. Martin lifted his robed arms up toward heaven and said in his deep preacher tones, slow and sure, *"And now unto Him who is able to keep you from falling and to present you faultless before the only wise God, our Father. Amen."* It meant, among other more important things, that church was over.

And this night, as always, the benediction finally came—the sound of the train clattering through our narrow space between the great mountain peaks, its whistle echoing after it. Living in Vienna, I missed the sound of the train sometimes, especially when I couldn't sleep.

Once again it worked its magic, because I didn't hear anything else until the storm woke me up.

Both wooden shutters banged against the window, torn loose from their latches by the wind. Rain poured in the still open window.

"Good grief!" Mom said, bursting into my room. Her long flannel nightgown flapping at her feet, she latched the shutters and closed the window. "You can sleep through anything," she said. "It's a great storm, Con, our favorite kind, with lots of noise and drama."

"I guess the church bells were right," I mumbled sleepily.

Mom leaned over and kissed my forehead. "It's nice to be back, isn't it, son?" She sat down on the edge of the bed. "Do you still want to live here so terribly, like you used to?"

I thought about it. "No, not so much, I guess. It seems different this time."

"You're growing up. And sometimes visiting old memories can be confusing. Don't worry if tomorrow is bittersweet, okay? And I promise not to provoke the Donners and ruin your day."

"Thanks, Mom. Night. And tell Da . . . Nigel good night, too."

Mom turned with surprise at what I'd almost said. She smiled as she closed the door.

It had surprised me, too. I certainly didn't mean to call him Dad. I liked him, but he wasn't my father. Even though all I had left of my real father was a faded picture in my wallet and one on the wall at Grandma Rea's house, he was still my dad. Someone exciting and brave and exactly the way I wanted him to be, a daring fighter pilot. Not a quiet, respectable business-man.

I thought about Nigel, though, how he had reacted today. If Mom hadn't been there, we would've given that Jag chase. I knew it. And he had acted so cool about keeping the guy trapped in that lane long enough for me to get a close look.

Maybe there was more to Nigel than appeared on the surface. Unable to go to sleep, I began to see things differently. Most of all the way he drove. It didn't fit his image. It was flat out—as if he had no nerves.

And then there was Nigel's office in our Braungasse place. I went over it in my mind. It was neat, like he was. Dark wooden bookcases covered three walls, filled with his old and rare books. He wouldn't let Mom put a curtain over the one tall, narrow window that looked over our courtyard garden out back and let in the morning light. On the other wall was an oversized framed map of the British Empire. It was old, and Nigel explained to me once that one like it hung in every schoolroom when his dad was a boy. All the countries in the empire were red on that map, and he showed me how the sun never set on it during Britain's heyday. Those were the days, he had said, when schoolboys were proud to be British and trained to rule the empire. But like all empires it eventually crumbled. Looking back on it, I felt sure he was sad when he said that. Nigel the patriot—trying to regain the glory days for England? Why not? It fit.

I bolted upright in bed. Of course he was more than he seemed. The quiet, brainy businessman was a cover. Nigel was a spy. A British spy. Why hadn't I seen it before? I reached beside my bed for the list of suspects stuffed inside my Asterix book.

I crossed off the Martins and all the others except Branko and Nigel. On the reverse side I wrote *Nigel A. Kaye. Physical Characteristics: tall, thin, good-looking. Most often dressed in a business suit and trench coat. Behavior Pattern: works long, ir-regular hours; travels often in the Middle East and former com-munist countries. Opportunity: unlimited contact possibilities.*

Qualifications: very intelligent; speaks German, French, Russian, and an African dialect or two. Further new cover: wife and son.

How could I have been so blind? The evidence was over-whelming. Gregor and Hannah could help me find the proof. *Nigel must have special equipment hidden in his office, or maybe there are some special features on the BMW that we could find.* Wow. Nigel and Branko. Life was certainly looking up.

I went to sleep for the second time that night, wondering if Mom knew she'd married a spy.

6

ESCAPE FROM GROSSGMAIN

As it turned out, Herr Donner wasn't even home when we first arrived. Frau Donner greeted me with wet kisses in her hallway, which, as always, smelled of cabbage. The smell followed us up the three flights of stairs as she led the way to our old attic loft, bowing to Nigel in a nervous attempt to please.

He had to duck to get through the doorway and could just barely stand up straight inside. Smooth as always, Nigel tried to put Frau Donner at ease. I saw Nigel in a new light today. He seemed much more interesting to me now that I suspected him of leading a double life.

Sunshine flooded into my old room as I opened the inner shutters, and with it came the memories. It seemed like another life, even though I had lived here a mere two years ago. The storm had moved on during the night and left a crisp fall day outside, clear and beautiful. But the old air trapped inside was damp and cold, and I shivered in my now bare and empty room. I missed the mess and wished we weren't seeing the place like this.

At least the view was the same. Up on the side of the mountain, the remains of an old medieval castle—Schloss Plainburg— still stood watch over Grossgmain. And on a peak just out of sight was Hitler's Eagle's Nest—history all around, ancient and modern.

"This your room?" Nigel asked, interrupting my thoughts.

"Yeah. Not as fancy as our Braungasse place," I said, feeling for some stupid reason that I needed to explain.

"Oh, I don't know," Nigel said in his slow and thoughtful way. "I haven't seen many views to match this one. And I imagine you managed to mess this room up as creatively as you do the one at home."

"Yeah," I said proudly. "Of course, there were those who thought Mom was crazy to live here when she could have had a great house back in the States. . . . Most of all my dad's—er . . . ah . . . my other dad's parents thought she was very strange."

Nigel smiled, not smug exactly, but as if he understood, which bugged me for some reason. He couldn't understand about my father. I didn't even want him to.

"You must admit," I changed the subject, "that Mom is a little strange—nice, but strange."

"Quite strange," he agreed. "Actually, it's my favorite thing about your mom."

I wasn't sure if he was putting me on. It was hard to tell with Nigel.

"Come on," he said. "Show me the rest of the flat."

The "flat," as he called it, was really just two rooms with a long hall in between. The front room tripled as the living room, dining room, and Mom's bedroom. It had the other window. I showed Nigel that view, pointing out the church beside the Vortel and the shops. I named the mountain peaks for him.

We stood there for a moment, looking over the beautiful little village and towering mountains. Like a postcard, people always said. And now it seemed unreal to me, too.

When we lived here, this room was cozy and warm, the walls lined with books and lithographs by Mom's favorite Austrian artist, Kasimir. Like my room, this one had since been repainted chalk white. Stark and empty.

"You should've seen it then," I said lamely. Finding it impossible to explain, I went looking for Mom.

She was pinned against the wall near the door by Frau Donner, who was rocking back and forth on her heels, talking nonstop. Donner's wife looked short, square, and drab next to my thin mom, who looked very American in her Levi's, Nikes, and bright yellow cotton sweater. True to her word, Mom was smiling sweetly at Frau Donner as though fascinated by whatever she was rambling about.

Wondering what Nigel must be thinking of all this, and realizing too late that my idea to come back and show it to him had been a mistake, I pressed on quickly, wanting to get it over with.

"Here," I said, spreading my arms wide, "is the rest of the flat. There's more than meets the eye in this hall."

I opened a door on our left. "This, as you can see, is the shower, with—I might add—a washbasin." I closed that door with a bang.

"Off to our right is another door. That is the WC, and we will leave it for the end of our tour. This wide spot in between is the kitchen."

Our old two-burner stove and half refrigerator were still there. Herr Donner had built Mom two cupboards above the stove. I could remember him working on it and playing with me while he did so. Nigel propped his long frame against it now, looking as out of place as anything. Too tall by half.

"Last, and certainly least," I went on, "is the WC. This bathroom's so small we had some guests who complained they couldn't even turn around in there and had to move crablike in and out." I demonstrated to an appreciative Nigel.

"Mom is a real genius at decorating, though," I said. "She put a life-sized poster of the one-eyed Israeli military hero Moshe Dayan right here on the wall. He just stood there in his battle fatigues staring down at you with one eye."

Mom had finally moved away from Frau Donner and walked up to us. Nigel grabbed her arm and said under his breath, "I say, Roberta, why did you have Moshe Dayan in the bath-room?"

"He wouldn't fit anywhere else," she said as though it were a perfectly normal question and answer. "A friend picked the poster up in Israel," she explained, "right after the Six-day War in '67 when Dayan was such a hero. It's a classic poster—I still have it. Would you like it in our Braungasse bath?"

"Don't look at me," I said, throwing up my hands. "It's her nicest quality. Remember?"

Herr Donner suddenly burst into this somewhat bizarre lit-tle scene. The door slammed against the wall with force, his presence filling up the space.

"Guten Morgen," he boomed, lumbering over to shake my hand. Leaning against the wall to catch his breath from the ex-ertion of climbing the stairs, he continued. "Nice to see you all again so soon. How do you like the place, Herr Kaye?"

Herr Donner was a very big man, nearly as tall as Nigel but much heavier. What must once have been muscle was now fat, particularly evident this morning in a tight pullover shirt and no jacket. His thick, bushy hair was completely white, un-combed now, and he smelled of alcohol. Herr Donner was drunk. It made the pockmarks look deeper in his flushed face.

"Shoot," I said under my breath quietly. *Why did I want this trip down memory lane anyway?*

Now that her husband was here, Frau Donner became very quiet.

She stared at him, and it wasn't exactly a look of love. Mom still smiled. But the smile was thin, and you had to be drunk or a fool to miss the coldness.

Nigel greeted him with a warmth I didn't think he felt. I remembered that spies had to pretend a lot. *He's probably good at it*, I thought.

Herr Donner turned back to me, leaning down in my face to talk. His low German slurred by drink sounded funny to me, and his breath was awful. I felt myself wanting to pull back—and hating myself for it.

"Ready for that ride on my new motorcycle today, Con?" he asked, beginning to laugh. "Only I think you had better drive."

No one else laughed.

Knowing there was no way Mom would let me go out with him in this condition, and still not wanting to hurt his feelings, I said, "Sure. Just like old times, eh?"

"That's right," he said. His words were slightly slurred, and he had to pant for breath. "And I have a new Mercedes to show you."

There was an uncomfortable silence for a moment when no one knew quite what to say. Then Herr Donner began fumbling in his pants pocket and pulled something out.

"Oops," he said. "I almost forgot. I have a special treat for you today." He repeated the word *special*—slurring it—as he took my hand and turned it palm up. I saw a flash of gold as he dropped something onto it, closing my fingers over a cold, surprisingly heavy object.

"Thank you," I said, as I had done last night for the candy he had given me in the same manner and as I had done a thousand times before as a young child.

Like a statue come to life, Frau Donner bolted toward us across that tiny room and with lightning speed whisked the object out of my hand before I realized what she was doing or even had time to see what, for a split second, had been mine.

"What are you doing? You crazy old drunk!" she shouted in his face. He grabbed her wrist and easily took the object back, sputtering very colorful German at her.

"This is mine. I earned it, and I will give it to Constantine if I want to. Besides"—he shook the shiny object in her face—"there are more in that old box. Enough for even your greedy soul. Now shut up!" His face contorted with anger. I had never seen him like this before, and it scared me.

"Keep it," he said, shoving it into my jacket pocket. "And don't listen to her." I expected that to be the end of it, but surprising even him, I think, Frau Donner continued to attack, swearing and then pounding him with her fists.

Herr Donner kept retreating until Mom, Nigel, and I were alone in the room. We stood there, stunned into silence. The rancid smell of sweat and alcohol lingered behind them along with shock waves from the violent eruption.

Their shouts retreated down the stairs, dimming in the distance, but not lessening in their intensity. Then the door to their first-floor apartment slammed shut.

Finally Mom spoke. "That was unbelievable," she said. "They always fight and fuss, harmless noise mostly. But . . . this . . . seemed serious. . . . Whatever is that thing?" she said. "Let me see it, Con."

From below, we could dimly hear the fight continuing. I handed it over. It didn't look valuable enough for all that fuss, at least not to me.

"Whatever it is, Roberta," Nigel said, "Con should certainly give it back. At once. No matter what it was about."

She didn't answer him. She didn't move. She just stood there staring at it, the blood draining from her face, making it the color of the walls.

"What's the matter? You look as though you've seen a ghost," Nigel said, putting his arm around her.

"Yeah. What's wrong, Mom? What is that thing, anyway?" I took it back for a closer look. It was a small, heavy gold box with fancy carving and a little door that pulled open. Inside was a tightly rolled scroll. Mom removed the scroll and gently spread it open.

I had seen something like this before, or similar to it, but for a moment I couldn't remember where.

"A mezuzah," Mom finally answered in a funny voice. "And a very beautiful one at that. A solid gold mezuzah."

"That's right, a mezuzah," I exclaimed. The Goldbergs had

one on their door. Only it was made of wood with a very modern design. From Israel, Hannah had said.

"Did you say solid gold?" I asked. "As in hundreds-of-dollars-an-ounce type of gold?" Tossing it lightly in my hand, I tested its weight.

Mom didn't answer; she just went on staring at the scroll.

"Are you sure it's a mezuzah?" Nigel asked. "It seems highly unlikely that Herr Donner would have—"

Mom interrupted. "Wanna bet?"

"Surely not." He went on. "And even if so, he would not give it to Con. . . . You must be mistaken."

"Oh, it's a mezuzah all right." Mom walked over to the light still streaming in my old bedroom window, and holding up the scroll, she read: " 'Hear, O Israel: The LORD our God, the LORD is one.' "

Mom's hands shook, making the thin, old parchment rustle as she explained. "That's the Shema. It is the watchword of Israel and the beginning of the passage from Deuteronomy that is written on every mezuzah scroll. The text goes on with the command to love the Lord your God and to serve Him with all your heart and with all your soul. The scroll even includes the reminder from Deuteronomy that these words are to be upon the doorposts of their house. Oh, it's a mezuzah all right. The question is, where did Herr Donner get it?"

"Who cares where Donner got it—that's his business," I said quickly. "He said he earned it. And he gave it to me . . . so it's mine."

"No," Nigel said. "He was obviously drunk, and it wouldn't be right to keep something this valuable under such circumstances."

"Come on. He wasn't that drunk. Give me a break. He knew what he was doing," I argued, wanting it more and more. "He's always doing that sort of thing. It's no big deal."

Mom went on studying the scroll, not moving away from the light. Then she dropped it away from her eyes and said,

"This is not right." Mostly to herself, she went on to explain, "Something has been added after the biblical text. It seems to be carefully written to look like part of the passage from Deuteronomy . . . but even I can see that it isn't. I wonder what it could be?"

"Can't you read it? I told you all those years of Hebrew study were a waste of time," I said lightly, trying to lighten up the atmosphere. It didn't work.

Nigel looked on patiently—waiting.

Finally she rolled the scroll just as carefully as she had unrolled it and replaced it in the mezuzah, firmly snapping it closed. Then in a ready-to-take-charge kind of voice, Mom said, "I'm sorry to disagree with you about this, Nigel, and in principle, I don't. However, I want Con to keep the mezuzah. In fact, I insist that he keep it."

I couldn't believe my ears.

Putting it in her purse, Mom said, "I'll take care of it for you, Con. You know how you lose things."

It looked as though Nigel was going to argue, but with a noncommittal shrug he touched her elbow and moved her toward the door.

Suddenly Mom was in a terrible hurry to get out of there without even a last look around. We closed the door behind us. It clicked resoundingly down the smelly stairway.

I didn't know it then, of course, but I would never be back, never be welcome in this house ever again.

The Donners' argument was evidently over. They were no longer in sight or hearing as we came down the stairs past their doorway.

Outside, we turned away from the street and walked along a path beside the house to another house much like it, set back behind Herr Donner's yard. He owned it, also, and we were going there for lunch with our very best friend in Grossgmain, Frau Maria Rozstoski. We called her Mia.

Although Mia was no relation, I saw Frau R. more often

than my real grandmothers in the States, and I loved her like a grandmother. But I wasn't in the mood to see her until I'd at least said good-bye to the Donners. It didn't seem right, the way we had left, practically sneaking out.

"Can I go back, only for a few minutes? I'll catch up with you long before lunch is ready, and Frau R. won't mind. Please?" I jumped up, touching the wind chime hanging from a covered bench in the garden. It made a nice tinkling sound.

"Stop it, Con. Don't draw attention."

Mom sounded nervous and jumpy. "No, you can't go back. I don't want him to change his mind about the mezuzah or have it changed for him."

"Come on. You know Herr Donner never listens to his wife. He isn't going to ask for it, not after he made such a fuss about giving it to me."

"Well, we're not going to take the chance."

We waited on Frau Rozstoski's doorstep with Mom nervously looking back at Donner's house as though she were afraid he might appear at any moment.

"Ring the doorbell, Con. I want to get in before they see us."

I groaned, unable to believe this—I tried again. "Five minutes? Just give me five minutes."

"No. You may not go back today. In fact, I want to leave Grossgmain right after lunch."

Nigel and I stared at her. "Leave? Now? Saturday noon? After all our plans for this weekend—all the things we were going to show Nigel? Why would we do that?" I demanded.

Nigel didn't look too pleased, either, and he said in a tight-lipped voice, "Could I talk to you alone for a minute, Roberta?"

"Wait, Nigel. Please. Mia will be here in a minute to answer the door, and I think I can explain better after I've had a chance to talk to her. I do have a reason. A good reason. Trust me. Okay?"

Pleading wasn't a tone I often heard from my mom. But she sounded so upset that Nigel hesitated only a minute before caving in.

"You'd better have a good reason," I muttered. "I can't believe you're so uptight about this mezuzah business. What's the big deal?"

Fortunately for me, Frau Rozstoski opened the door at that moment. Very old, and bent over a metal walker, she still managed to look like the aristocrat she was.

"Meine güte, Constantine, my littlest angel." She patted my arms as I hugged her.

"Not very little or angelic anymore, I'm afraid, Mia." Mom said it with a little laugh as she in turn bent down to hug the thin shoulders.

Mia greeted us all warmly, and the tension disappeared. It was good to see her.

Nigel had only met Frau R. briefly, when he and Mom got married. Her only living relative, a brother who lived in Vienna, brought her to stay with him so she could attend the wedding.

Nigel took her hand and brushed his lips lightly against the wrinkled old skin.

She beamed, leading us into the familiar sitting room. It looked like a *Masterpiece Theatre* set. Nigel, at last, appeared completely at home.

◆

Frau R. looked like a relic from a very distant past. Which she was. Funny old Mia. She came from a time before McDonald's and didn't know the meaning of finger food. It was a great lunch of hot homemade noodle soup and crispy bread. The trouble with Herr Donner seemed to be forgotten. At least it wasn't mentioned. A distant relative of the royal Hapsburg family, Mia told Nigel some of my favorite stories of her life, including visiting Schönbrunn Palace with her family as a child when Europe still had kings and queens.

"Tell Nigel about how you had to run away to England in order to study medicine—because your family thought it was beneath you."

"I think perhaps we should leave the past," she said graciously. "I do not want to bore my guests. Tell me about the bright new day in eastern Europe. What hope do you see for those poor people, Nigel? They lost so much under communism."

He took his usual time but answered carefully, "It will take a long time, and things are very difficult politically and economically," he said. "And time is about all they do have at the moment. That and their new freedom. By the way, last month I was in Czernowitz—but I'm afraid I didn't see anything of your old home. Is the castle still standing, do you know?"

"Nigel!" Mom said shocked. "You didn't tell me you were there."

Before he could explain to Mom, Frau R. excitedly began asking questions about her childhood town. She was the oldest daughter of a very rich and powerful baron. Their estate included most of the town of Czernowitz, which was still part of the Austro-Hungarian Empire—then it was Romania—now it is in the Ukraine.

I had heard her tell stories about these places since I was a little boy. And while I usually loved to hear them, all I could think about now was the fact that Nigel hadn't told Mom about that trip. *What other trips has he made?* I wondered. *And what besides business does he do on those trips that he doesn't tell Mom about?*

"I haven't been back to my home on the River Prut nor seen the beautiful Carpathian Mountains since we were dragged away at the beginning of World War II and forced to live in horrid places in the once beautiful city of Bucharest—which the Communists also managed to befoul," she said bitterly.

Her hatred for the system that had killed most of her family, taken their land, and imprisoned her for many years was still strong. Her frail, old body trembled at the memories.

Nigel listened intently but felt my eyes on him and finally said, "I say, did I forget to put something on today, Con? You're staring at me in the most unusual manner."

Catching myself, I mumbled something under my breath and asked Frau R. to tell him how she finally got out of Romania and came to live here, right behind us.

"Oh, that was a happy day!" she said, her wrinkled face beaming. "Con was a little baby, and Roberta helped me move in. I can't do much with this back of mine." She looked fondly at Mom, her eyes moist. "It had been so long since I had seen beauty or could trust someone to be my friend. And I never would have been allowed out of Romania without the help of our good family friend, the archbishop of Romania. He had to endure the wrath of the Securitate, the secret police, but finally Archbishop Milea prevailed. After I was out, my brother chose Grossgmain for me because of the clean air, peace, and quiet."

"Nice of the Communists to let you go after you were too old and ill to work anymore," Mom said sarcastically. "Too bad the overthrow of Romania's cruel dictator, Ceausescu, did not come many years before."

"How did you injure your back?" Nigel asked as we finished Frau R.'s special homemade ice cream.

"An especially rough interrogation," she said simply. "Ceausescu's thugs broke my back. But enough of all that." Getting up she said, "Let's have some coffee and talk of happier things."

Later, Nigel and I were alone while Mom helped Mia in the kitchen. Nigel wandered around looking at her bookshelves.

I was getting antsy and ready to go. "I think I'll go to the kitchen and speed them up. Maybe Mom has changed her mind about leaving. She doesn't seem upset anymore."

Nigel turned to me and in an uncharacteristically firm way said, "No, I don't think you should bother them now. They want to talk alone."

"Oh no! Not that mezuzah stuff again. I hope Mom isn't telling Frau R. about that. It isn't her business."

I followed Nigel out onto the balcony. The doors had been standing open while we ate, letting in the warm noon air. The balcony was lined with window boxes full of still-blooming geraniums only slightly damaged by last night's storm. The balcony overlooked Herr Donner's house, and I could see my old bedroom window. There was still no sign of the Donners.

"I don't know exactly why your mother is so upset about this, Con," he answered after thinking for a moment. Nigel always seemed to think very carefully before saying anything. "But whatever it is, we should give her the benefit of the doubt. She isn't the kind of person, generally, to overreact. Is she?"

"No. I guess not," I had to admit. "But it doesn't make sense. Mom wanted to come as much as I did."

"Then there must be a very good reason to leave."

I wasn't ready for reason, so I ignored that. "I do know this. Mom and Frau R. don't like Herr Donner. There was some kind of ruckus the last year we lived here. He tried to have Frau R. thrown out. I don't really know what happened. It died down, but Mom never liked him after that . . . after all the nice things he'd done for us. I think it stinks."

Nigel was standing beside me, leaning on the railing.

"What exactly had he done for you?"

"Well, he was . . . our friend . . . and let us live there. I mean, we paid rent, but he always seemed like more than a landlord." I was finding it hard to explain. Embarrassed, I went on. "I know it looks bad, after today . . . but you saw the other side of him last night. And it wasn't always so bad. He didn't used to drink so often. He was my friend, Nigel. What can I say? Are you supposed to stop liking someone because they aren't perfect?"

I turned my head to meet his eyes, which gave away nothing. He wasn't making this any easier.

"You don't have to explain," he said. "And you are right.

Remembering is important. Loyalty is a fine quality. But, Con, now that you're getting older, you must learn to mix it with reason."

There was a nagging feeling in the back of my mind. Like when you know an answer on a test but just can't quite nail it down. My frustration at Mom's unreasonableness and the thought of a lost weekend must have kept me from whatever was tugging at my mind. There were things about Herr Donner I had been ignoring. Little pieces I didn't want to put together. I stood staring gloomily at a bright red geranium inches from my nose.

Finally Nigel said, "Herr Donner and Frau Rozstoski don't like each other, I take it?"

"You take it right. And it's more than dislike."

"Well, they're from very different social classes. Being British, I understand that. Perhaps it's natural that they feel uncomfortable and mistrust each other. Their roles have been reversed. He is still a peasant, in the old sense of the word. But one with money. Her kind of social class and status is one thing his money cannot buy."

"Maybe. But what bugs me is that Mom and Frau R. don't think he has a right to the money somehow. I don't see what business it is of theirs, no matter where he got it."

"Look at it logically, Con. You are actually a brilliantly logical lad. Think—don't feel—for a moment. Where did a man like that, with nothing before the war, come up with enough money to buy up expensive property here in Grossgmain? He's a rich man. Don't you think it's possible your mom and Frau Rozstoski know something you don't? Something that causes them to feel the way they do?"

Frustrated, I walked back inside and plopped down in a big, comfortable armchair. Standing on a table beside it was a picture of Baron Rozstoski and his wife holding a baby in a long white christening gown. The picture was faded and torn at the corner. I knew this picture was the only thing Frau R. had left of her parents. Like the pictures I have of my dad.

I sat staring at it. *Why do I feel guilty? Mom is acting weird, and I feel guilty.*

Nigel came in and sat down across from me, looking earnest. "I know you must be very upset about all of this, but on the basis of past performance, I'm asking you to trust your mom and do what she wants. Without making it difficult for her."

"The least she could do is tell me what's so blasted important about that thing," I exploded.

He took his usual time. "Some things cannot be explained, not for a while, anyway."

Just then the door opened and Mom carried in a tray of coffee. Mia had fixed me a cup of her special rich hot chocolate with cinnamon-dusted whipped cream on the top. She took it from the tray and balanced it for a moment on the frame of her walker before handing it to me, saying, "For the littlest angel, as I used to call him, because he brought light into this old lady's life after years of darkness." She kissed the top of my head and set down the cup, stumbling a little as she did so.

Nigel jumped up to help her, but she brushed him away kindly. She could walk short distances without the walker and continued to do much of her own work with pride and dignity.

"Constantine was like a grandchild to her, Nigel," Mom explained.

"*Is* like a grandchild," Frau R. corrected her. "Wars kept interrupting my life and I never married," she went on. "I didn't mind that so much, except I missed having children. But when I moved to Grossgmain, I found not only the long-awaited liberty but love, as well. A gift. A wonderful gift from God."

Mom looked all teary eyed. Everyone was quiet as we drank. I thought my separate thoughts as I finished the creamy, dark chocolate.

Finally Nigel stood up and took Mia's hand. "Thank you for a wonderful meal and a memorable time. I have looked forward to this with great anticipation. But we must be going now in order to be back in Vienna in time for Con and me to make it to the Kino tonight. He has been wanting to see an American film playing there, and tonight is the last chance we'll get."

Mom looked at Nigel, visibly relieved, and then nervously at me to see my response.

"Will you walk with me, Con?" Mom suggested, not very sure of herself for a change. "We could go out the back way and through the woods to the pension to pack our things. Nigel can get the car from the Donners' driveway, then pick us up there."

Frau R.'s piercing gray eyes looked at me with love and a little pressure. Mom looked at me with something a little more like pleading. What could I say?

"Okay, Mom, let's go." Everyone beamed, and I felt a little guilty because I was tired of this trip down memory lane and ready to go home, anyway.

Nigel said his good-byes and left for the car. After he was gone Frau R. walked with Mom and me to the door. She gave me a hug, and the familiar smell of fine face powder and starched clothes filled my nose. I hugged her carefully, aware of her fragile body.

"Come and see us in Vienna soon," I said. "We have an apartment on the first floor now. And you should see it—it's a lot bigger than that one." I pointed to our old apartment.

She had never been in our loft, right next door, because of all the stairs.

"Thank you, Mia, for everything," Mom said, giving her a final hug. "Call me if you think of anything else that might help. Or if you find that letter—send it at once."

"I will, dear," she said to Mom. "And be careful. Please be careful." Her tone was urgent, her rather severe face full of worry.

We turned and waved to Frau R. as we started down the path outside her back door.

I knew why we were walking this way, why Mom didn't want

to pass the Donners' house. She still thought he might stop us and take the mezuzah back. That part was easy to figure. What I didn't know was why she wanted it so badly that we were literally escaping from Grossgmain with it.

◆

It was eleven o'clock Saturday night when Nigel and I returned from the movie. The Clint Eastwood Movie Festival playing at the Burg Kino had attracted Americans in Vienna, who like to see any movie in English, and Austrians who have a thing about old Eastwood Westerns. Gregor was there with his dad, and I saw half the kids from AIS, too. I left thinking Dirty Harry's mean stares had nothing over Ms. Gaul. Nigel and I enjoyed the evening, never mentioning Grossgmain. I looked at him in a new way now. His potential hidden life seemed much more interesting than doing business, and I couldn't wait to get on with finding out what it was.

The phone was ringing when we walked in the door. Mom must have been asleep.

"I'll get it," I shouted to Nigel.

It was Frau Rozstoski.

"Don't wake your mother," she said. "I have a message for her. Con, this is very important. Tell her I found the letter and mailed it so she would receive it Monday morning. You will remember, won't you, Con?" she exhorted me before hanging up.

I groaned inwardly, assuming it was about the mezuzah again, but assured her I wouldn't forget and went off to bed. My thoughts were quickly consumed with Dirty Harry and Nigel as James Bond and how rich I would be when Mom got over her fit about the mezuzah and let me sell it. I made a mental note to look up the price of gold tomorrow. I should have added a mental note about the letter.

TOP SECRET

7

THE PLAN GOES DOWN

IT WAS SUNDAY EVENING AND THE THREE OF US WERE SITTING on our small balcony. Mom and Nigel commented occasionally on the setting sun changing the color of the trees and other poetic stuff. A few cars crept slowly past toward the Vienna Woods. No fast red Jaguars, of course. No cute girls, either. I didn't know anyone cuter than Hannah, anyway. My mind wasn't really on cars—or girls for that matter—but on Nigel and the very interesting plans I had for Monday.

A few Sunday-afternoon stragglers were still making their way down Braungasse after their walk in the woods. The men carried their wives' purses in that strange Austrian custom understood only by them. Somehow I couldn't picture Nigel carrying anybody's purse.

He looked relaxed leaning back in his chair, his long legs stretched out on the balcony railing. He was reading some papers out of the briefcase beside him. *Boy, is he cool*, I thought. *No one would ever suspect him. No one, that is, but me!*

Nigel had been very quick to agree when I begged off our usual Sunday-afternoon soccer—he had "stacks" of work to do, he said, preparing for a trip to Poland tomorrow.

So . . . Gregor, Hannah, and I spent the afternoon in the bakery. Sometimes Branko let us use the front of the shop when it was officially closed if we told him we needed some private space. We thought it would be a good opportunity to "get a feel for the bakery" and see if any interesting people showed up.

Hannah and Gregor had agreed that Nigel was an interesting target for our search. We would concentrate on Branko later if Nigel proved to be a dead end.

That afternoon while Nigel got ready for his "business" in Poland, we planned how to uncover his cover.

Mom was curled up on the bamboo-colored wicker couch pretending to study Hebrew for class tomorrow. In fact, she kept inspecting the scroll from my mezuzah over and over, then picked up her Hebrew dictionary, then her Hebrew Bible, then the dictionary again. Usually nothing made Mom happier than just such a quiet time to read or study. But she didn't look happy now. Not since yesterday morning when the mezuzah business started. Tense and jumpy with me, she seemed especially close to Nigel, and he fussed over her as though she were sick or something. Who could figure parents?

Even in church this morning I saw her making notes that didn't appear to be on Rev. Martin's sermon.

My mind went back over the scene in Grossgmain. Frau Donner's wild attack on her husband had been so different from her usual nagging. Maybe fear had made her attack him like that. Maybe she knew something her husband didn't know or that his morning beers had made him forget. *Why did he have to get drunk the day I visited?* I thought for the thousandth time. *In front of Nigel.* I was still embarrassed at how they had acted in front of him.

The quiet and my thoughts were interrupted by the ringing of the phone. "Don't get that," Mom said as I jumped up to answer it.

"What. . . ?" I started to argue but decided against it.

Mom was right about one thing. Frau Donner had convinced her husband that giving me the mezuzah was a bad idea, and now they both wanted it back badly. During lunch Herr

Donner had called twice asking if they might come to see us on Monday. Mom had managed to tell them very firmly no, and in my mind, not very kindly.

Mom nervously avoided my eyes as the phone rang unanswered. Nigel made no move to answer it, either.

I let it ring. *It's Mom's problem.* I had more important things on my mind. Tomorrow's plan was missing one small piece. I needed a ploy to keep me home from school.

Whoever was calling us finally gave up.

I'll be glad when Mom gets over whatever is bothering her about the mezuzah and gives it back to me, I thought. She was "just keeping it safe for the moment," she had assured me.

I went back to concentrating on my problem—how to get time to search Nigel's office without either Mom or Nigel in the house. Tomorrow was perfect—Nigel out of town, Mom at the university all day. I would be "sick" and stay home from school. Hannah and Gregor would join me to search the place.

"No surprises, Con," Hannah had insisted as we discussed it at Branko's. "Not that I mind skipping school exactly, but this'd better work or my parents will kill me—not to mention you, because I'll tell them it was totally your idea," she cheerfully assured me.

"What could possibly go wrong?" I had asked them, only to receive very skeptical looks from my two loyal buddies.

Well, it was going to work. Now if I could just figure out how to convince Mom I was too sick to go to school.

Hannah's escape would be simple because her aunt Lucy from New York was staying with her while her parents were on a quick vacation in Italy. Hannah would leave for school at the regular time, only instead of walking to the bus, she would walk a little farther down Braungasse to my house, where I would be waiting. Fortunately for her, Aunt Lucy hated to answer the phone just to hear someone rattle off German she couldn't understand. So she didn't answer the phone while Hannah was at school. When the school office called by nine-thirty to say Hannah hadn't shown up, no one would answer. The next day Hannah would forge an excuse note from her dad to explain her absence. Piece of cake.

Gregor did this kind of thing all the time—no problem, he assured me. He would arrive shortly after Hannah, as his school started later. Gregor's mom might be easily fooled. Mine wasn't.

The trick was to be sick enough to stay home but not sick enough to keep Mom home from the university. "Healthy unless proven otherwise" was her rule.

I was counting on the fact that Mom hated to miss her day of Hebrew. *We should have plenty of time to search Nigel's office and the BMW,* I thought as I went over our brilliant scenario yet again. Nigel didn't like to leave his car in the airport parking lot when he traveled, so he always took a cab to the airport. "We might not have this chance again for weeks," I had argued to convince Hannah and Gregor. Hannah—the techie of our group—would use her computer skills to check out Nigel's PC while Gregor and I checked out the rest of his office and the car.

I looked at my watch—I had one hour. If Hannah and Gregor didn't hear from me by eight o'clock, the plan was on.

Deep in scheming, I hadn't paid attention to Mom and Nigel quietly talking about his trip until I heard him say, "No, Roberta, I won't be at the trade fair in Warsaw the entire time. I have a little traveling to do. You can't call me, so I'll call you."

"Anything in particular going on?" Mom asked in a polite but not terribly interested tone.

"Not really," he answered smoothly. "There are a few problems that need to be stepped on."

I gasped out loud—shocked at Nigel's bluntness. They both turned and looked at me quizzically.

"I finally figured it out," I said, pounding my pencil on the notepad I was holding. "Ms. Gaul will be proud."

"You've been studying?" Mom asked skeptically.

"Sure," I said. "What'd ya think I was doing?"

"It looked far too intense for homework," Mom said, but she had already lost interest and was back into the Hebrew books in her lap—or mentally back in Grossgmain.

Trying to smother my excitement, I went back to my problem more convinced than ever that I must find a way to stay home tomorrow. Nigel even talked like a spy. I looked at his feet casually resting on the balcony. *I would hate to be a problem Nigel needed to step on.* I shivered a little.

Blood. Blood would be effective. But was it worth a tiny self-inflicted stab wound to a nonsensitive area? I'd considered that kind of thing once before but couldn't go through with it. Besides, knowing my mom, she would bandage it up and send me off to school anyway with a lecture about being more careful.

Brown eye shadow rubbed under my eyes to prove over-tiredness would get me a lecture about going to bed earlier. I'd tried that one before—at a much younger and simpler age.

Gregor had suggested swallowing a raw egg after breakfast. Great for producing evidence all right, but the very thought of it nearly produced some evidence right there on the table in the bakery when he suggested it.

I finally decided to use the simple and painless instant fever routine.

"Want a snack with me?" Nigel asked, putting his papers carefully back in the briefcase and flicking the small gold combination lock to secure whatever was inside.

"Nah," I said, staring at the briefcase lock and wondering how I had missed all these clues before.

"What? No to food? You must be sick." Nigel stretched as he stood up. "Never known you to turn down a perfectly good spot of food."

I jumped at my chance. "Well, as a matter of fact, I don't feel so good," I said. "Probably a virus."

"Probably—you spent two hours at the bakery this afternoon," said my cynical mom.

"It would be dumb to miss out on the rest of those sticky buns and cider, Con," Nigel urged.

He looked surprised when I didn't leap to join him. Mom stood up to go with him. Patting me on the head as she went past, she said, "Not to worry. Con might be many things, but dumb's not one of them."

As I sat there, the sun finally went out of sight and the air turned cold quickly. *Hope Mom is right about me not being dumb*, I thought, letting the tiniest little doubt about tomorrow creep in.

Eight o'clock came and went. I made no calls. It was on. I continued to build my case the rest of that evening. Since it was hard to look sick instead of excited, I stayed in my room most of the time, refusing any food.

It was kind of fun having a James Bond–type for a dad, I decided, imagining what he might be doing in Poland besides going to a trade fair. What did England want from their spies these days, anyway? I wondered what he would tell me if and when I confronted him with the evidence to prove his undercover work.

I felt a twinge of guilt when Nigel stopped by my room to say good-bye.

"Hope you feel better, Con. And by the way, thanks again," he said. "You showed real maturity yesterday. I was proud of you for leaving Grossgmain without a fuss. I know how much that trip meant to you."

"No problem," I mumbled. "Have a good trip. And take care of yourself."

"Righto! Not much danger in being a businessman, is there?"

Rationalization soon overcame my guilt, and I went to bed happy on a Sunday night. This was one Monday I was looking forward to.

◆

Next morning I produced a nice 101-degree fever using the hot-water bottle hidden under my feather tick.

Enough evidence to keep me home, but not enough to keep Mom home with me, I thought.

"What do you mean you don't want me to stay home alone?" I choked, panic coming over me when Mom responded totally out of character. "I've stayed home alone lots of times. . . . And I'm not that sick. It's only a little old 101 . . ." I was rambling.

"I'm sorry, Con. You cannot stay here alone today." It sounded like a final answer.

So why, I thought nervously, *does she have to pick this day to act like a nervous mother?*

"I don't know why you chose today to get sick."

I didn't think I should answer that one.

"Well, you'll have to come along and wait in the car. There's no other way. I won't be long." She said it firmly, her mind clearly made up.

"Come along?" I choked again. "I might as well go to school as sit in the car all day."

Maybe I can catch Hannah on her way over here if I leave quickly—then we can still catch the bus. Panic began to set in.

"I'll just go to school," I said, getting out of bed.

"No, of course not. You can't go to school with a fever. It's out of the question." Mom's voice was shrill and strained. "It will be warm in the car. I'll skip Hebrew class, but I have an important appointment I can't miss this morning. Come on, get your jacket, a pillow, and something to read. We'll even take Nigel's car. I'm sure you'll be comfortable in it."

"Really, no, Mom. Let me stay here. Please!" I hoped the desperation in my voice would be interpreted as pain. Which is what I would experience if Hannah had to stay outside all day waiting for three o'clock so she could go home. At least Gregor would go back home and make up most anything when he failed to find us.

"You'll be fine. Get your things together and take a Tylenol," she said, leaving my room. "Get a move on or I'll be late."

I moved. Apart from telling Mom why I didn't want to go with her, which didn't seem like a good idea, there was nothing left to say. I had to go. And Hannah was certainly going to kill me.

Getting into the car, I began to feel genuinely sick. I lay down in the backseat and groaned. *How do I get myself into these things?*

Reason returned when we stopped at the bakery and Mom ran in for rolls. We hadn't had time to eat breakfast—not that I minded—and a warm Berliner sounded good.

Hannah will have to forgive me, I reasoned. In time. It wasn't my fault, after all. There was no way in the world I could've known my mom would go soft on me. And if Hannah had her key, she could go in and look around without me.

The thought of spending the morning in the car and missing school for the day, kicking back for a couple hours with the Sony, cheered me up no end.

I leaned over the seat to get my Discman, which Mom had grabbed for me on our way out. It was next to her purse. She had left it open on the seat, taking only some change. I could see the mezuzah, the gold shining up at me, tempting me to pick it up. *It's mine after all*, I thought, but then the door of the bakery opened and Mom was hurrying to the car.

"Branko said hello, and he hopes you feel better," she said. The wonderful smell of Branko's baking filled the car. "I'm sorry to bring you out like this." Mom handed me a sack of Berliners. "You should be home in bed. Are you feeling any better?"

"Yeah. Great," I said, biting into the warm pastry. "Good—

I mean, not too good. But better, definitely better. Probably the Tylenol," I stammered.

"Your appetite seems to be unaffected," she said a few minutes later, looking at me in the rearview mirror. "That's your second."

"Tylenol are amazing little things, aren't they?" I answered, trying to look a little less comfortable. I put in a U2 CD, slipped my earphones on, and closed my eyes. Wondering briefly where we were going, I was tempted to eat a third Berliner.

"Take off those earphones a minute so I can talk to you," Mom interrupted my thoughts some time later.

I sobered up and realized we were in the old city. Down near Saint Stephen's Cathedral.

"Who do you know down here, Mom?"

"Oh, terrific!" she said, ignoring my question. "A parking place right in front. First time for everything."

Finding a parking spot in the old part of Vienna was no small miracle. These streets had been made for horses, not cars, and parking was always a problem.

"It seems to be getting colder," Mom said. "I think I'll get you that blanket Nigel keeps in the trunk."

The day was Vienna gray and it looked like rain.

Mom tucked me in like a kid and fussed nervously as if she felt guilty. "Are you sure you'll be okay?" she asked. "I'll leave the keys in the car, but don't put down the windows or open the sunroof. Do not come in unless it's an emergency. But—but if you truly need me, I will be on the third floor, the room right in front of you as you step out of the elevator. There's a sign on the door, *Dokumentationszentrum*. I won't be over an hour. Take care, dear."

"Okay, already. Would you stop fussing and go on?" *What's the deal?* I wondered again. *She never acts so nervous. And what is she going to do in a documentation center?*

Mom was gone before I could ask any more questions. Besides, I was more worried about Hannah. It was getting colder fast. Where was she going to spend the morning? Key or no key, she probably wouldn't dare go into our apartment, not knowing what was going on or if Mom was there or when we might return. *And she never carries any money on her,* I thought miserably, *so eating and riding the tram are out. She's going to kill me for sure.* And to make matters worse, it was starting to drizzle.

Hannah told me later what happened. . . .

Hannah went as agreed to the apartment, waiting across the street for my all-clear signal from the kitchen window.

But no signal came. There was no sign of Gregor, either, and no movement in or out of the apartment. The BMW was gone, but the Fiat was still there. Thinking my mom might be late leaving, Hannah figured she should stay out of sight—just in case. She stepped behind the old linden tree directly across the street and tried to look inconspicuous to passersby. The key to our apartment was in her pocket, but using it without knowing what was going on inside was too scary. So she waited, growing ever more upset with me.

The postman came, leaving a letter in our mailbox by the door buzzer. Still no sign of anyone, still no signal from the kitchen window.

Something had gone wrong for sure, Hannah decided and began to wonder what she should do—and why she always let me talk her into these wild schemes.

Just then she noticed a large Austrian man in Tyrolian clothes approach on the other side of the street. The heavy, slow-moving man walked up to the gatepost and pushed the button beside *Kaye.* When there was no answer, he rang again and again, pushing the buzzer harder in frustration.

Out of breath from walking, the old man had to lean on the gate while he waited. He pushed the buzzer again. Still no answer.

The man looked familiar to Hannah for some reason. Moving a little bit away from the tree, Hannah tried to get a better look, but the man continued to face our apartment and she was unable to get a clear view of his face. What she did see startled her.

Reaching into the postbox, he took out the letter the postman had only moments before deposited. He held it close to his face as though struggling to read the envelope. Then he let out a string of obscenities, ripped it open, and read it. Hannah couldn't believe his reaction. Right there in the middle of Braungasse, he shook the letter in the air, hitting his forehead in frustration and finally stuffing the letter in his pocket. He turned to cross the street, and Hannah finally saw him, his face full of rage.

She jumped back behind the tree, but it was too late.

He saw her watching him and strode quickly across the street.

By then Hannah knew exactly who he was—Herr Donner from Grossgmain. She had met him only once, but she hadn't forgotten his pockmarked face.

Hannah started to walk off, pretending not to notice the old man coming toward her, but it was too late. Herr Donner reached out and took hold of her left arm above the elbow.

"Hey there," he said. "Do you know the Kayes? An American family who lives in 49A?" he asked with forced friendliness.

He wasn't exactly hurting her arm, but when Hannah pulled, he tightened his grip and looked more closely at her face.

"Of course you do. You are Con's friend. You came to Grossgmain with him once. Didn't you? Yes . . . yes. I remember your name . . . Goldberg." He said the name with a sneer.

Hannah's heart sank. He must have known she saw him take the letter. Desperate to avoid any more questions, Hannah pulled harder to get away. But Donner did not remove his big, hairy hand, and it was beginning to hurt her arm.

"Well, do you know where the Kayes are?" he asked, no

longer pretending to be friendly. "I must see them right away. I have just put a note for them in the mailbox. It is urgent that I find them right away, you see?"

Hannah had seen. She saw him take a letter out of the mailbox and read it—not put one in. She also knew Donner must be there to get back the gift he had given me over the weekend. She wondered why I had been so vague about what it was and why Herr Donner wanted it back. But it hadn't mattered much before. Now it did, and she wished she knew what on earth the gift was and why he wanted it so badly. But why would he take and read our mail? There was desperation in the man's attitude and the same cold dislike she had felt before. She wasn't exactly afraid, yet the desire to get away from the old man was growing. But he had not loosened his grip on her arm. She was thinking of another way, but she didn't know how to do it.

Hannah didn't need to lie to him about us, although she would have been glad to do so. However, she really didn't know where we were and said so.

Frustrated at not getting what he wanted, Donner became even more threatening.

"What were you doing waiting outside their house? How long have you been here? You should be in school at this hour, with Con. Maybe you are meeting Con here and both skipping school. Is that it?" He was talking close to Hannah's face, his breath was terrible, and he panted as he talked, as though gasping for air. "Why doesn't Con answer the bell—is he inside waiting for you?"

Hannah was beginning to feel more angry than afraid. His Bavarian accent made it hard for her to understand even his fairly simple sentences. She thought she had understood most if it and couldn't believe he had the nerve to hold her against her will.

"I have to go now," Hannah said and tried once more to pull away. But Donner didn't let go.

"Why don't you wait right here with me, little girl? I have

a feeling if I stick with you, you might just remember where Con is." It clearly wasn't a question—it was an order.

Herr Donner leaned against the tree and pushed Hannah down hard on the curb in front of him. "I don't want you to get tired," he said maliciously.

He didn't want her to get away, either. Where was Frau Schnively when you wanted her? Hannah thought. She could call out to her, and Donner wouldn't dare keep her with a witness.

But no one came. Not Gregor. Not Frau Schnively. Not anyone. So much for nice, quiet Braungasse.

Frustration and the rain finally drove Donner to action. "I need in that apartment, girl. You wouldn't happen to have a key, would you?"

Hannah's fingers tightened around that very key, deep in her Levi's jacket pocket. She began to sweat despite the cold. What could be so important to drive Donner here, make him steal our mail, and now be willing to break in to get it back?

Hannah shook her head, trying not to look afraid. "Why should I have a key?"

Donner hesitated and looked for a moment like he might search her for it. Then he grumbled, "Ja, ja. I suppose not. Why would they give you a key?" The way he said "you" made Hannah's skin crawl. "I need a drink. Where is the closest Gasthaus?" Donner asked menacingly.

"A long way," Hannah lied, hoping Donner didn't know about the one just around the corner. He couldn't have or he wouldn't have asked, she reasoned, desperately wanting him to believe it. This was her chance to try what she had thought of as her best possible escape. She took a deep breath and went for it.

"But there is a bakery right up the street. You can get coffee there."

"That's not the kind of drink I mean," Donner snarled. "I don't want a bakery. . . . I want a drink."

"Well, that's all there is unless you want to walk down past the tram stop several blocks."

The thought of walking very far in this cold drizzle, even for a drink, was clearly not welcome.

"Okay. We will go to this bakery. But you remember something, little lady: You are coming back here with me. Together we are going to find Con if it takes all day."

He pulled her roughly to her feet, and lowering his grip to her wrist, he twisted her arm up behind her back and shoved. It hurt, but she wasn't about to give him the satisfaction of begging him to stop. Now that they were moving, her chances of getting away before he tried to break into our apartment were better. She was afraid of being alone with him behind closed doors. And if he looked he would find the key. She knew she had to get away from him, and she knew Branko would help.

Donner kept a tight hold on Hannah's arm, pushing her in front of him as they walked. He was struggling to breathe again when they reached the bakery. There was only one customer, and she was taking her time, carefully choosing two of these, three of those, and one half of something else, all the while talking away between choices to Frau Loveric.

Hannah's heart sank when she saw Frau Loveric instead of Branko.

Donner released Hannah's arm as they entered the warm, friendly bakery. He sat down heavily on the little chair at the table right by the door, making sure she couldn't get past.

"Go and get me coffee," he ordered Hannah. "And a Semmel."

Hannah walked over to the counter praying Branko was somewhere in the back room baking. She didn't know Frau Loveric and didn't know if she would act quickly enough to help.

Finally the other customer was finished and Hannah ordered, deciding at the last minute to order some hot chocolate and a hard breakfast roll—a Semmel—for herself. She had been too excited this morning to eat and decided she might need her strength before this was over. After ordering, Hannah lowered her voice and said, "Where is Branko? I need to talk to him. I am a friend of Con's and I'm in trouble." She knew she had jumbled her German and wasn't sure if she had made herself clear, but she couldn't risk saying any more. Donner noticed Hannah's lowered voice and was quickly beside her at the counter.

"What did you say to her?" he growled.

"I just ordered the food—like you said."

Frau Loveric looked closely at Herr Donner. Hannah knew she would notice his clothes and realize that he was not from Vienna.

Frau Loveric smiled sweetly at Hannah as she set about getting the order together. She asked no questions and gave no clue as to whether she had understood Hannah's plea for help or not.

Herr Donner couldn't very well draw attention to them by refusing to pay for Hannah's roll and hot chocolate, but he gave her a very black look as he laid down the 150 Schillings.

Back at the table, Hannah began to breathe more easily. And thanks to the hot chocolate and Semmel, the cold began to leave her body and she stopped shaking.

Donner sat close and stared at her from inches away. "Maybe you didn't understand me. You are going with me to find Con, so don't try anything stupid."

Hannah tried to make her Semmel last a long time, hoping that Branko would show up. But no one came, not even another customer. Frau Loveric had disappeared into the kitchen and had not come out again. Hannah watched the door to the kitchen, hoping desperately that she was getting Branko.

"Why do you want to see Con?" Hannah decided she needed to delay Donner, who had noticed the rain had stopped and began gathering his things to leave. She had to stall him, get him talking. Branko had to show up sometime soon.

"Come on," Donner said, ignoring her question. "You are going to help me get in that apartment. Maybe you will talk to their landlady and convince her Con left something for you there. Anyway, the rain has stopped and we are going. I do not have time to waste sitting here talking to a Goldberg."

Donner's tone of disgust as he said her name did not escape Hannah. Herr Donner had stopped panting for breath and regained his strength. Frau Schnively might just let them in, Hannah thought, and she had never been so frightened as she was now at the thought of being alone in the apartment with him. "I'm not ready to go yet," she said, staying seated.

Herr Donner stood up, throwing the little chair back against the wall. His massive body towered over her as he grabbed the hood of her sweat shirt, pulling her hair with it as he hauled her to her feet.

At that moment Branko walked in. Herr Donner was side-tracked for a second by Branko's entrance, and Hannah pulled away as Branko moved quickly around the counter toward her.

"Good morning," he said in his friendly way. "And why aren't you in school this morning? Not sick, I hope, like Con. You two looked all right when you were in here yesterday."

Donner looked furious at this intrusion and sensed what Hannah had done by bringing him here for coffee and whispering to that woman. He moved toward Hannah, trying to catch her arm. "Let's go," he said.

Branko stood between Herr Donner and Hannah and gave no indication of moving.

Hannah looked at the phone behind the counter and asked to use it.

"Go right ahead," Branko replied.

Branko was as tall as Donner, twenty years younger, and much more fit. With obvious effort Herr Donner changed his approach.

"When you are through on the phone, we'd better be going." He sounded as nice as anything.

Branko looked at Hannah.

"Fräulein Hannah, would you like to stay for a while?"

Holding the receiver, she heaved a big sigh of relief. "Boy, could I use another cup of hot chocolate!"

Branko laughed. "Sorry, sir. My friend is going to stay. Why don't you come back later?" He held the door open for Donner.

Donner made a move toward the counter, but Branko, still holding the door open with one hand, blocked him with his other.

The old man had no choice and he knew it. He stared for a moment at Hannah, then at Branko. Muttering furiously, he stomped out, practically knocking off the little bell above the door as he slammed it closed.

"Now, Hannah," said Branko, turning to her. "I think you'd better tell me what all this is about."

Relief made her knees weak, and Hannah leaned her back against the wall and slid down, hitting the floor with a thud. The phone receiver dangled beside her.

A HIT AND A MISS

HANNAH'S TROUBLES MIGHT HAVE BEEN OVER, BUT MINE were just around the corner. Bored with searching for hidden gadgets in Nigel's car—which was "clean" anyway, except for a few Berliner crumbs here and there—I turned my attention to the building Mom was in.

It had been over an hour since she'd entered the old-fashioned wooden door directly across from me. The building looked, and probably was, centuries old. A decorated, hand-painted sign in old German script hung over it from heavy iron hooks. The faded letters said *7 Seitenstettengasse*.

Beginning to feel nervous at the long delay and unable to sit still, I stepped out of the car to stretch my legs. The sky was gray and still dripping—old, drab Vienna. With my Discman turned off, thoughts I had been avoiding forced their way through the fog in my mind. Things were nagging at me. Like Mom's reaction to the mezuzah. And forcing me to come along with her instead of letting me stay home this morning.

What is she afraid of? I wondered. *And what is she doing?* The word *Dokumentationszentrum* bothered me. I had never heard of any such office before. It had nothing to do with the university or her studies. A center for documents. *So what on earth is that? What kind of documents?* The same questions went around and around in my mind.

Not able to come up with any answers and getting cold to boot, I decided to get back in the car. But while I was still leaning over its top, staring in a useless fashion at the door underneath the number 7 sign, I noticed two men walk up and open it. One man went in quickly; the other taller man held the door open as he looked up and down the street, then across at me. He met my eyes, paused for a moment, then followed the other man inside.

Whoa—that's funny, I thought. Here you had your classic spy scenario. Open trench coats with collars up and heads down. Those two were nervous and in a hurry, one covering for the other as they moved into the building. Very professional.

I got back in the car, shuddering involuntarily from the look in that guy's eyes. He reminded me of someone. Someone with a tight, pinched face and cold eyes. Dirty Harry. He looked like Dirty Harry in the Clint Eastwood movies—lean, mean, and tough.

Wondering vaguely what "Dirty Harry" and his friend were up to in the same building as Mom, I went back to watching passing cars for excitement, trying not to think. A well-honed skill, Mom would have added.

I could see about half a block each way before Seitenstettengasse curved out of sight. The old city was built more or less in a circle, with an outer-ring type street around it. The small inner streets twisted and turned in all directions without pattern.

Seitenstettengasse wasn't a major shopping street, but a steady stream of cars kept passing, looking, no doubt, for parking. So at first I didn't find the white Audi strange as it cruised by several times. It was a new Audi Quattro. I noticed it especially because it had a small neat line from front fender to rear door as though a nail had been carefully drawn across it. It caused me great pain to think of a scratch like that on our BMW. The Audi had a *D* sticker right above the license plate, which had call letters similar to my date of birth, March 28. *MAR 280* read the German tag. *Plenty of German cars in Vienna*, I thought. *No big deal.*

Except that when the car parked in front of me pulled out and the Audi went right by without even hesitating, I knew whatever he was looking for wasn't a parking place.

Engrossed in the white Audi, and worrying about what Mom was doing, I didn't notice the two old ladies walk up to my window. I jumped when they knocked.

"Was willst du?" I shouted at them in German through the window. "Scare a guy to death," I muttered under my breath.

"Good heavens . . . so sorry. We didn't mean to frighten you, son," said the larger of the two. "We want to ask you a question."

Her accent was definitely American, and she was talking in that v-e-r-y s-l-o-w way often used with children and foreigners. To my trained eye, these two were retired American school-teachers—tourists of the worst kind. They had on polyester pantsuits and flowered blouses with big floppy bows. They were without umbrellas, and the drizzle soaked nicely into the polyester, making blobs of darker color and frizzing their bluish hair.

I turned the key and lowered the window. It would have been amusing to play with them—languagewise—but I didn't have time to chat and my nerves were shot. I had decided to go in and check on Mom despite her orders to stay put. The white Audi cruised by again and this time slowed down right in front of number 7, hesitating until the honking of horns finally made it move on.

This was the kind of suspicious behavior Hannah and I had trained ourselves to look for. But I had a general sense of unease rather than excitement, and talking to two little old ladies didn't help my nerves.

They were blocking the car door, practically leaning in the window and both asking in insistent teacherly tones, "Son, do . . . you . . . speak . . . English?"

"Most of the time," I drawled, using my western accent and

pushing the door open at the same time. "But I'm in a hurry."

"Now, listen to me, son. There is no need to get huffy; we only want some directions," she said, tugging on my sleeve as I locked the door. I didn't care what Mom said about waiting. I was on my way in.

The white car had gone around the block again and was stopped directly in front of the door, traffic piling up behind it. This time the driver ignored the honking and rude gesturing.

Over the noise in the street and the continuing questions from the polyester pair about how to find this wonderful little shop—down in the catacombs . . . where you can buy real Austrian wicker furniture—I heard a sound like a muffled explosion and felt a slight tremor. Even the annoying women shut up for a minute. We all looked around, unable to see what might have caused it.

"Excuse me, I have to meet my mother," I interrupted as I started across the street.

And then it happened.

Out of the door charged Dirty Harry and friend. The wind blew his trench coat open revealing—I couldn't believe it—an Uzi machine gun in his right hand, obviously meant to be hidden under the flap of his coat. Whipping open the door of the Audi with his left hand, he hesitated while the other man got in, looking once more up and down the street and then across at me where I stood not six feet from him, staring into those cold eyes. He raised the gun toward me for a fraction of a second, and then the car began to move and he was forced to jump in or be left standing.

It was all over in a few seconds. The car screamed off, tires sliding on the wet pavement as it turned the corner, out of sight. The backed-up traffic began to move, surging forward after the frustrating delay.

Dashing between the cars, ignoring the insults hurled at me, I made it across the street. Something had happened inside that building, and my heart pounded from fear.

Praying that Mom was all right, I punched the button of the ancient elevator, tried the locked stairway door, then in panic and frustration held the elevator button down. Leaning against it with all my weight, I waited, thinking I could hear sirens coming in the distance.

Finally the elevator arrived and time began to move again, but not fast enough. Just as the doors of the elevator closed, I saw police burst into the building, guns drawn.

The old elevator groaned and bumped upward, leaving the cops in the lobby. It jarred to a stop at the third floor, the smell of smoke and a scene of destruction greeting me as the doors opened.

The Dokumentationszentrum sign wasn't there. It must have been blown away with most of the door. The hall was littered with glass, and I could hear people crying and the sound of the police pounding up the stairs in their heavy boots.

Vaguely I realized they were storming through the stairway door—locks hadn't slowed them down. Ignoring their drawn guns and shouts for people to get down, I ran into what was left of the room, shouting wildly for Mom.

"Get down," a policeman yelled again, giving me a shove downward, forcing me to my knees.

"They're gone," a stunned young woman said. Her face was full of fear, but she looked unharmed.

The police lowered their guns at that—their tension eased a notch as they moved into the smoke, broken glass, and shattered furniture.

Tears and smoke blurred my vision as I stumbled to my feet. My chest hurt and I was having trouble breathing. *She's not dead*, I tried to tell myself. *She can't be*. Looking through the chaos, I realized nothing else mattered, not any of these other people, not anything but her. I heard myself calling her name, aware that a medic was talking to me.

"Looks like you'd better sit down," he said. I was trying to tell him about Mom when I saw her.

While looking through the rubble for clues, the police had moved a big, heavy desk a few feet in front of me. Crouched behind it and kneeling in a pool of blood, Mom was covering another body with her own.

"Mom!" I screamed. "Mom."

She looked up, tears running down her cheeks and mixing with blood from a cut above her eye. "Oh, Con," she said. "I'm not hurt. I'm okay . . . but . . ." Her words trailed off as she looked down at the man whose head she was holding. "Look what they have done to Herr Wiesenthal."

It was his blood making the pool on the floor, soaking her Levi's. His head rested on Mom's arm. I had never seen the man before, but the shock of all this horror and the relief that Mom was not seriously hurt made me weak, and I dropped to the floor beside her, afraid I was going to throw up.

Slowly the rest of the room came into focus. Mom continued to hold the man's head until the medics reached him. They moved her and put him on a stretcher. Their almost wild actions and quick, shouted commands to each other confirmed my fear that whoever he was, he was about to die.

Mom and I looked on helplessly until finally the stretcher was carried out.

Others were wounded, and the medics examined Mom when the more seriously hurt were taken care of.

"This needs stitches," a medic told Mom, looking at her forehead. "I will close it with a bandage now, but they will fix it properly at the hospital and check you thoroughly for other injuries."

"I don't have any other injuries," Mom said, resisting his effort to lead her to the door. "I will see my own doctor later. Right now I want to talk to the police . . . not sit in some hospital."

"They will come and take your statement there," he said gently, probably used to people in shock refusing help.

"No." The answer was firm, and it sounded to me like she

was not in shock but rather very much in control. "Time is important, and I will talk to the police here. Now."

She said it in a tone of voice I knew so well, and the medic did just what I would have—obeyed her. He went off in search of more willing victims.

We sat there together, leaning up against a still standing pillar.

"Why?" I asked. "What's happened? Why are you here?"

"Later, Con . . . later. It's going to be okay. I'll explain . . . when I can. Now I have to speak with the police. I won't be long. Wait for me, son." She stood up—a little jerkily—and moved away, leaving me completely confused and utterly shaken.

I waited for nearly an hour while throngs of police with endless forms continued to question Mom and the other survivors. Mostly I wandered around in a daze, watching policemen dig through the rubble. Finally I perched on a windowsill trying to sort it all out in my mind.

It was becoming clearer what had happened. Dirty Harry and friend had shot their way in, blown up some files, wounding those nearby, and shot Simon Wiesenthal, the old man Mom had been holding, whose name everyone seemed to know. Why my mom had been there in the first place was bothering me more and more.

From where I was sitting, I could see the cars continue to drive up and down Seitenstettengasse. People were craning their necks to see what was going on in number 7. Police cars still blocked much of the street, making the traffic worse than ever.

I could also see the BMW parked across the street. The memory of looking for spy gadgets in Nigel's car seemed more than a little silly now.

"He's a fool, that's what he is."

How'd they know? I wondered, turning my attention back inside the room to see if I was the "fool" in question.

A uniformed policeman was ranting as he dug a bullet out of the wall near my foot, but he didn't seem to be referring to me.

"Wiesenthal thinks he can go around stirring up hornets' nests and not get stung." He went on. " 'Famous Nazi-hunter' nothing. Decent Austrians are sick of old Nazi stories. The fool didn't know when to shut up, and somebody decided to do it for him. That's what I think."

"So you said, Willie. Why don't you keep your opinion to yourself and do your job? If Detective Sinnbrunner hears you talking like that . . . what with press around and"—he looked up at me—"others around to hear you. You'd better keep your yap shut. You'll be demoted back on the street beat so fast we won't even see you go."

Clearly unwelcome there, I pulled up a chair near Mom and listened to the ongoing questioning. She no longer looked weak and vulnerable. Her tears were gone, replaced by a seething anger that shocked me. Blood had stopped dripping from her forehead, and the stains on her clothes were drying. An aggressive plainclothesman pushed her for answers. Another non-uniformed man, younger and very well dressed, stood behind him, occasionally giving orders and answers to the remaining policemen as they finished up.

"How long have you worked undercover for Herr Wiesenthal, Frau Kaye?" he asked in what seemed to me an unfriendly and highly suspicious tone.

I laughed. No one heard me or took any notice. I stopped laughing when I heard her testy reply.

"I don't think I wish to answer that question now," she snapped. "I'm not sure it's any of your business and quite sure it isn't relevant to your investigation into all this . . . horror. Why don't you stop worrying about what I did for Herr Wiesenthal and try to find out who shot him?"

Stunned at her response, I shook my head in disbelief. What on earth was the man talking about, and why didn't she just give a simple answer? I wanted desperately to get out of there and go home. Relief at finding Mom unhurt was replaced with something more like anger and confusion.

She noticed that I was listening and came over and put her arm around me. "I'm sorry, Con. We can go now." I wondered what she could read in my face since I didn't even know what I was feeling.

Chief Detective Sinnbrunner, the well-dressed man who had been listening to Mom's interrogation, joined us, introducing himself. Younger than many of the others, he was slightly built but spoke with authority without bluster. Since he had arrived a short while ago, the investigation looked less chaotic.

"Your mother said you were waiting outside in a car when all this took place," he said to me.

I nodded.

He looked directly into my eyes. "This is very important," he said, his face showing no emotion. "Think carefully before you answer and then tell me all you remember. Did you see two men leaving the building shortly before you came in?"

I didn't have to think. It was all very clear, especially the eyes of the man with the gun. I could even see the women who had distracted me, keeping me at least from running directly into Dirty Harry's arms as he came out the door.

"Yes, sir," I replied fairly matter-of-factly. "Going in and coming out. Plus the car that picked them up."

He swore under his breath, looking at Mom questioningly.

She nodded. "If he says he saw them and the car, then he did see them. And he never forgets a car—notices everything about them—if they're expensive, that is."

"Didn't any of your men think to question this boy earlier?" Sinnbrunner asked a uniformed man beside him, who mumbled a non-answer while looking at his feet.

"Get back in here. We're not through yet!" he yelled at a few officers who must have sensed it might be a good time to take their leave, including the two guys I had overheard talking about Wiesenthal.

Now all of the attention—the forms and questions—were directed at me.

I carefully described the men. They had worn ski masks when they entered the room, so it turned out no one else had seen their faces. Sinnbrunner was an Eastwood fan, too. He smiled at my description of Dirty Harry.

"We'll be able to make a sketch from your description." The detective didn't hide his excitement about the information I gave.

"Now, what do you remember about the car? Exactly. And take your time."

"Let's see . . . it was a new white Audi Quattro. There was a small, neat scratch on the passenger side from front fender to rear door." I watched Sinnbrunner's assistant take down every word. I was starting to enjoy this.

He looked at me a little skeptically now and said, "You didn't happen to notice the license plate number, did you?"

"Yes, sir, I did. And I remember it, too. It was a German tag. His *D* sticker was right above the plate. *MAR 280* was the number. It stuck in my head because my birthday is March 28." I felt downright cheerful. Finally some of the trivia I continually stored in my brain was proving useful.

Sinnbrunner glared at his men, and with cold sarcasm he addressed them: "Thanks to your incompetence, overlooking the best eyewitness in the room, you have given the terrorists at least an hour's head start. They could be halfway to a border by now."

No one moved. No one responded.

"Well, don't just stand there! Move!" he yelled at them. They moved. He went on shouting at them, frustrated by the knowledge that once the car crossed the border, there was little chance of getting the terrorists.

"I suppose you noticed the color of the car's interior?" he asked.

"Yes, as a matter of fact, it was light blue."

He groaned. "I don't believe this."

"It did go around several times," I explained. "And like Mom said, I do notice cars. And I've made a habit of watching for things to happen."

"Too bad he didn't see the weapon. He would have recognized that, also," Mom put in.

The Austrian policeman looked doubtful.

"Good grief . . . I forgot the Uzi," I said, hitting my forehead. "The one I called Dirty Harry—he had an Uzi. I saw it when the wind blew his trench coat open."

Sinnbrunner slapped me gently on the back. "You're all right, kid." He smiled for the first time.

"He does see things," Mom said. "And remembers. I just hope he's as good at . . . at understanding things."

I didn't like to think what she might mean by that. Sinnbrunner looked confused, too, and he turned back to me.

"You know, you really have been a big help. Frankly, we rarely catch professional killers like these. But with your help we have a shot at them. Thanks." He put out his hand, and I shook it with my practiced steel grip.

"Sure," I said, wishing a few more people were there to hear the compliment.

"That about wraps it up for now. I will send one of my men to drive you home via the hospital, Frau Kaye. You are in no shape to drive. Another officer can follow in your car."

Before Mom had time to argue, and I knew she would, I asked him, "Will you need me to make an identification when you catch them?"

"Probably so. But we will make sure it isn't during school hours. I'm sure you're the kind of boy who hates to miss school." He grinned. "By the way, why aren't you in school today?"

"Oh my goodness! I totally forgot. How are you feeling, Con?" Mom reached over and felt my completely cool forehead. Her hand was shaking and she looked faint. My worry about her returned. "We'd better go now. He's sick and should be home in bed," Mom said, adding guilt to my other emotions.

It was still gray outside, but the rain had stopped. I went to the BMW and got the blanket Mom had put over me. She was shivering in the backseat of the police car that was to drive us home. A phone call to Dr. Reiks asking him to meet us at the house convinced the police to let us skip the checkup at the hospital.

I covered her with the blanket, remembering why she had given it to me earlier. I knew I had to tell her. "Mom . . . I have something to confess to you. I wasn't really sick today,"

"What?" She looked puzzled. She shivered under the blanket. "Never mind now. Whatever it is, it can wait. I'm so tired and so worried about Herr Wiesenthal. . . ." Tears filled her eyes and she seemed fragile. "I have some explaining to do, also. Things you will have to know now."

Worried and confused, I was glad to put it off. "Okay . . . no hurry."

I sat very still beside her as we drove through the busy city streets on the way to our more remote neighborhood.

Mom looked so small, lost under that big blanket pulled up to her chin. Her head leaned back against the seat, eyes closed.

I had never thought of Mom as weak or defenseless, but she looked that way now with her hair all messed up and spots of dried blood in it. The skin on her forehead was thin and white— I could see the blue veins standing out. The white bandage on her cut was stained dark red. I could smell the smoke in her clothes and what I thought was the sweet odor of blood.

Slamming on his brakes to avoid a tram, our driver swore and turned around to see if we were okay. Mom's purse fell off the seat, dumping all its contents on the floor of the car, but

Mom only stirred slightly, not even opening her eyes.

I bent down to pick up the things from her purse and felt around to make sure I got everything. *That's odd*, I thought, checking again all over the seat and floor. The mezuzah was missing. I knew I had seen it there this morning—at the bakery.

I looked at Mom, wanting to ask her about it, but I didn't have the heart to wake her.

I leaned back against the seat in real tiredness and defeat. The harder I tried, the less I understood.

We were going past the little Volksoper, the People's Opera House, and there was a line at the ticket window. Smaller and much less grand than the State Opera House, ordinary folks loved it, and the traffic jam around it slowed us down. I watched the faces of the people, normal ordinary people, and thought of Dirty Harry's eyes, cold and murderous. There was so much I couldn't figure out, but this one thing I knew for sure: I would never forget that look, that face of the man who had almost killed my mother. I hoped that I hadn't left such a strong impression on him. I remembered Sinnbrunner's close questioning about whether or not the terrorists had seen me when I had seen them.

How could it matter? It wasn't as if he knew my address. But I couldn't shake the fear of staring into those cruel eyes. I was very glad indeed that he didn't know my address.

"My address!" I said out loud, hitting my forehead. "I forgot to tell Mom about the letter."

"You all right back there, young man?" the police officer asked while looking at me in the mirror.

"Yes, I'm sorry," I said mostly to Mom, who had startled awake at my outburst. "Go back to sleep. It can wait, like everything else."

"No, go ahead. We're almost home, anyway. What letter did you forget?" Mom asked, sitting up a little and holding her head as if it hurt when she moved.

"I forgot to tell you about the letter! And Frau Rozstoski

said it was urgent. She called Saturday evening when we got home from Grossgmain. You were sleeping and I took a message. Only I forgot to tell you about it because Nigel and I left for the Kino. I'm sorry, Mom."

"What was the message?"

"She said to tell you she had found the letter you wanted soon after we left. She rushed it to the post office just before they closed and mailed it special overnight delivery so you would get it in Monday's post. 'In plenty of time,' she said. 'Plenty of time for what?' I asked her. But she said, in that voice you don't argue with, 'Never mind, Con. Give your mother the message. The letter will arrive Monday morning.' "

"Oh dear. If I had known that, I'd have waited for the mail this morning."

One more piece in a puzzle without a pattern.

"I'm sorry," I said, wondering if it might have prevented all this somehow if we had only waited. "It slipped my mind. . . . I didn't know it was so important." I knew—but didn't particularly want to say—that it had slipped my mind because my childish spy search scheme had taken up all available space.

"Don't look so upset, Con. Maybe it was for the best anyway." She sighed, closing her eyes again. "The letter is sure to be there when we get home. We can count on that. The Austrian post never fails, through rain and snow and dead of night and all that. I can read it in peace and quiet, just what I need after today," she said. "Peace and quiet."

AFTERMATH

THE LETTER WASN'T THERE, OF COURSE. NEITHER WAS THE peace and quiet.

Instead we were greeted by an assortment of policemen and half the neighborhood. Hannah was there along with her aunt Lucy, Branko, and Frau Loveric. Frau Schnively had let them all in—at the request of the policeman who opened our door for us.

"I think you'd better come inside, Frau Kaye," he said as if it were the police station and not our home he was inviting us into. His shock upon seeing our police escort matched our confusion at his presence.

After a stunned silence everyone started talking at once. Blood had dried on Mom's clothes, leaving dark brown stains on her Norwegian wool sweater and ruining her always perfectly white running shoes. Her Levi's were stiff from the puddle of blood she had knelt in, and the cut on her head had continued to soak through the bandage.

"This looks worse than it is," Mom assured everyone in a somewhat weaker than usual voice. "I was in the wrong place at the wrong time—Con can explain it all to you," she said, ignoring the protestations. "But what is going on here? Why are you here and with them?" she asked, motioning toward the three police officers now talking to the man who had driven us home. After asking everyone to stay put, the police officers moved into the privacy of our kitchen to use the phone.

Branko moved in front of Frau Schnively, who had been dominating in her usual fashion with irritatingly noisy questions. He took Mom's arm and moved her toward the hall tree. Stiffly she sat down on the covered cushion, dropping her hand over the carved wooden arm of the antique bench. As she did so, she knocked the umbrella stand to the floor. Tennis balls scattered everywhere.

While we picked up the bright green balls, both stories began to unfold. Leaning against the living room doorjamb, Hannah avoided my eyes, letting the adults do the talking. Branko told us about Herr Donner stealing our letter, holding Hannah against her will, and then proudly told us how she tricked Donner into the bakery for help. The police, in tracing Hannah's story, brought them here to finish the questioning—at the scene of the crime. Frau Loveric had been questioned as a witness, too. A very frightened Aunt Lucy had been picked up by the police and brought to comfort Hannah, and we had arrived in the middle of all this. Branko told the unbelievable tale with great precision, but I had the distinct impression he was being very careful, maybe leaving some things out.

I was speechless; Mom was horrified.

"Oh no . . . I didn't really think Donner would go that far. Hannah . . . are you all right? I'm so sorry." Mom was so upset that she failed to ask the critical questions, namely why Hannah wasn't in school, either, and why she was hanging around outside our apartment.

"Why, Hannah?" I managed to ask. "What did he want with you?"

"In. He found me waiting across the street and thought I could help him get in your apartment."

"Well, why call the police? I mean, it wasn't like he kidnapped you . . . just because he wanted your help." I felt Hannah had overreacted.

Hannah looked at me for the first time, her face reflecting confusion and hurt but not really anger. Branko started to reply, but I cut him off before he could defend her.

"Where's Herr Donner now? I'll ask him why he did it. He'll tell me and we can clear this up." My logical suggestion met no response.

It was true the letter was missing—why Herr Donner would want Frau R.'s letter was a mystery to me but hardly a crime. But could Herr Donner possibly want the mezuzah back badly enough to hurt Hannah? Of course not, I reasoned. He must have scared her because of his large size and rough manner. Everyone was overreacting.

I gave up. The scare with Mom, and now this. Sensing my discomfort, Mom changed the subject and briefly explained that she had been with Simon Wiesenthal when an attack was made on his life and office.

Clicking her tongue and continually tugging at her sweaters, Frau Schnively wrung her hands and flitted around the room, muttering about the shame to the neighborhood, of kidnappers right here on Braungasse . . . boys not in school . . . ruined reputations . . . and most of all, what was Mom doing in that "horrid man Wiesenthal's office, anyway?"

Despite her protests, I knew Frau Schnively was delighted. Her boring little life was suddenly full of enough gossip to last for years. I wished desperately that she would shut up and go away.

Finally Dr. Reiks arrived to take care of Mom. Not wanting to hear more, I followed her into Nigel's office, where the doctor calmly began to clean up the cut on her head, which turned out to be fairly deep and nasty. His fingers explored the bump on the back of her head, caused, she said, by a "flying hard object."

Mom sat weakly, resting her arms on Nigel's perfectly neat desk. She didn't seem to even notice what Dr. Reiks was doing. He asked very few questions but set about gently sewing up her wound. He had heard on the radio about the attack, he said, and unlike Frau Schnively, he did not criticize Wiesenthal. The radio account had included Mom's name as one of the "uninjured" survivors of the attack.

"You don't look uninjured to me," he said, but he knew better than to ask why she hadn't gone to the hospital.

"This head of yours should have been X-rayed," he concluded but didn't push it.

Mom seemed more worried about me than her head. Patting my knee and looking altogether worn out, she finally asked the obvious question.

"Why weren't you and Hannah in school? What did you mean about not really being sick today?"

I told her the whole thing—in English—so Dr. Reiks couldn't understand.

It sounded pretty stupid now, even to me, and Dr. Reiks raised his eyebrows as though he understood more English than I had thought. Mom smiled at my suspicions of Nigel and for some reason didn't seem overly upset at my deception.

"Son, son, when will you learn? You couldn't have known, of course, about the danger to Hannah. . . . But there is a real world out there, and the consequences could have been tragic." Her expression changed then—from the weak, tired look, back to the aggressive woman who had taken on Detective Sinnbrunner with such force.

"That man has done enough and must be found. It makes me sick to think of him hurting Hannah. Please hurry up," she said to Dr. Reiks with new determination. "I need to speak to the police again."

I had expected to be in big trouble with Mom for lying to get out of school. Confused by her reaction, I stared at the desk, now littered with surgical stuff, and expertly flicked cotton balls off into the wastepaper basket. Finally Dr. Reiks gave Mom a gentle hug on his way out the door. He might not approve of the activities that landed her in this mess, but his kindness and friendship seemed intact.

"Behave yourself now, Con," he said to me, not unkindly, it seemed, and with humor in his eyes. I had told my tale to Mom in English because I thought he didn't understand. So much for my assumptions.

Everyone but the police was preparing to leave as we rejoined them. All statements had been taken, all questions had been asked of Branko, Hannah, and Frau Loveric. Detective Sinnbrunner had arrived and was now huddled with the other officers in our kitchen. It looked like a police convention in there.

"I'm very sorry to have involved Hannah in this," Mom said to Aunt Lucy. "I'm so thankful she wasn't hurt. I would never have forgiven myself. . . . Please tell her mom and dad how sorry—"

"Please," she interrupted Mom. "Don't upset yourself. You could hardly know what the kids were planning."

"Wirklich!" Branko said. "So this is what you cooked up in my bakery yesterday afternoon?" He gave me a pat on the arm. "Con, Con, when will you learn?"

Where had I just heard that?

"Sorry," I mumbled, thinking at last about Hannah's feelings.

"I guess it's a good thing you stayed cool, Hannah, and didn't let Donner know you had a key. He wouldn't have done anything . . . but—"

"Key? What key? She has a key"—Frau Schnively pointed at Hannah in horror—"to my house?"

Everyone ignored her.

"Well, I was concerned about Donner showing up here," Mom said. "That's why I insisted Con go with me. Of course I didn't know Hannah would be here. It was very clever of you to go to the bakery for help. I guess you two know whom you can count on. I'm grateful, Branko," she said, her voice choking.

I walked out to the gate with Hannah. "I'm sorry about what happened today—glad you weren't hurt."

"It's okay. Just another one of your schemes gone wrong," she said lightly. But we both knew it was much more than that.

I stood outside in the dark watching everyone walk away and thought about what had happened today, here and downtown. It didn't seem real, any of it. It was more like a nightmare with all the right people in the wrong places doing crazy, weird things they would never do in real life. A real nightmare.

Back in the kitchen Detective Sinnbrunner was talking to Mom about the possible connection between Donner's attempt to retrieve the mezuzah and the hit on Wiesenthal.

Could Herr Donner have known about her connection with Wiesenthal's war-crimes investigations? Could he have arranged to have the files destroyed by Monday morning? Did he, in fact, have that kind of pull? Enough time? Were the events totally unrelated?

Back and forth Mom and Sinnbrunner went with these wild ideas.

Whenever the mezuzah was mentioned, Mom looked nervously at me, finally saying, "I will explain later, Con. Please wait." And since it didn't seem to me that I had a choice, I waited, thinking more and more that I was not going to like the explanation.

"Takes time to organize a hit like that, and Donner had no way to know—even if he was aware of your connection with Wiesenthal's organization—that you would take the mezuzah to Wiesenthal today," Sinnbrunner reasoned.

"But the recent successes of Wiesenthal's office, which probably prompted today's attack on him, must have made all the old Nazis nervous—including Donner. When he sobered up and listened to his wife, he realized how foolish he had been to give away something of that nature to Con and came back to get it. Right?"

"Probably. Probably but not certainly." Detective Sinnbrunner scratched his head and went on. "The only thing I'm certain of is that everyone in Austria knows Wiesenthal's office was responsible for bringing about the arrest of two men last month. Men wanted for war crimes who had been living right here in Austria for generations. Men who thought they were safe after all these years. Now that has made other old Nazis nervous, and stirred up new neo-Nazi activity."

I remembered the events at our school and wondered if that was the kind of "activity" he was talking about.

The phone rang before I could ask someone to please explain the connection between Nazis and Herr Donner—just because he gave me a little Jewish box.

It was Frau R. on the phone. She had heard a TV report of the attack and the mention of Mom's name as an "American, thought to be working for Wiesenthal, who survived the attack." After several moments of reassuring her we were both fine, Mom put Sinnbrunner on the line to hear the contents of the stolen letter—directly from Frau R.

I pulled up a chair and listened as he talked for several minutes, muttering, "Ja, ja, I have that, go on." Finally Sinnbrunner hung up the phone, obviously frustrated. He paced about the small kitchen, rubbing his hands while he talked.

"Donner saw Frau Rozstoski's return address on the letter he took out of your mailbox. He read it, and I can understand the violent reaction observed by Fräulein Goldberg. He is a desperate man now. . . . With evidence mounting, he won't go home tonight. Or ever again, probably."

"What do you mean 'never go home'? What will he do?" I felt my voice screeching. "What will he do?" I was horrified that somehow we had driven him from his home.

"Contact his Kameraden, the other SS officers that have kept an organization for such times as this. They will hide him or help him out of the country. If he is caught, they will pay his legal fees. At one time their organization was called the Odessa. Now who knows what it is called—we just know it is out there. And that it still has plenty of money in Swiss banks. Money that the SS stole from their victims and sent out of the country just in case. And now new funds are coming in from the growing neo-Nazi movement."

"Oh, they will take care of him all right," Mom said with hostility in her voice.

"What was in the letter?" I asked, unable not to ask but afraid I didn't want to hear the answer.

Mom answered.

"It was a copy of a document sent to Frau Rozstoski by her friend the archbishop of Romania—remember, Con, he is the man who helped get her out of Romania. Well, a German military attaché by the name of Johann Schmidt told Archbishop Milea the following incident. He even agreed to give it to Milea, who was only a priest at the time, in a sworn written testimony. He knew of Milea's personal interest in the fate of the Jewish population in his home region of Moldova and his desire to document what had happened to them. After the war, Milea took an even greater interest and compiled other evidence.

"The letter described an incident in 1940 in a bar in Bucharest. An SS officer with the rank of Second Lieutenant, Untersturmbannführer Donner, and his men were in this bar celebrating—it seemed—their transfer back to Germany. They were bragging about being so loaded down with loot from the Jews they had 'cleaned out' of Moldova that they couldn't carry it home."

"Donner *is* a common name," I ventured.

"Donner is a common name," Mom admitted. "And that's why when Frau R. received this letter two years ago, we knew there was no way to tell if it was the same Donner. Of course, when I read the files today in Wiesenthal's office, the war record showed Helmut Donner as serving in Bucharest during 1940 with the same rank—Untersturmbannführer—and that he was attached to the office of Hauptsturmführer Gustav Richter, the man in charge of the 'Jewish problem' in Romania. Then I knew for sure. And when Donner read this letter today, he knew, too, that we had nailed him."

I groaned as Mom, her face full of triumph, added, "All the pieces are fitting into the puzzle. And the mezuzah is the most important piece."

Mom and the detective were eager, excited, like hunters ready to pounce on their prey. I had asked Herr Donner once about the war and what he did. His answer satisfied me, then and now. *"Obeyed orders,"* he had said as cool as anything. *"That is what soldiers do, Con, obey orders."*

I knew it would be hopeless to try to convince Mom. This whole adventure had turned into a bad dream, or a movie in a foreign language where you see what is happening and hear everything that is being said, but none of it makes sense. And there were no subtitles to help.

"My spy," I laughed bitterly. "Some spy."

"What did you say?" Sinnbrunner asked me.

"Nothing, forget it," I mumbled.

"We will continue to watch the house in Grossgmain. Frau Donner might possibly lead us to him." Sinnbrunner gathered up his papers.

"You will try to find him, then?" Mom asked with a note of sarcasm in her voice.

"I resent that, Frau Kaye," the cool, efficient detective said. "I know that Austria's record of facing up to its Nazi past, finding and prosecuting Nazi war criminals, is not good; however—"

"However . . . that is a bit of an understatement considering Kurt Waldheim was president of Austria for six years," Mom interrupted.

"However," he continued, looking irate but choosing to ignore her barb about the former Austrian president who had been an officer in the SS, "as long as I am running this investigation, everything will be done to find the hit men and Donner. The acts of people like them make good Austrians look bad. I don't like that."

"I'm sorry. I had no right to suggest that you personally would look the other way," she said. "You must admit my concern is justified, though—about Austria's attitude."

He didn't deny it.

Finally it was over and we were alone. Nigel's office had contacted him in Warsaw, and he was on a plane heading for home.

The phone had been ringing off the wall, mostly concerned friends. In fact, Pastor and Mrs. Martin were on their way over with some hot food. We hadn't eaten since our Berliners that morning, and that was a long time ago. In more ways than one.

Gregor called to say he wouldn't be hanging around anymore. His mother was very upset to hear Mom was involved with "that man," and she didn't want Gregor influenced by such fanaticism. I think he sounded sorry, but it didn't seem to matter after everything else, and I supposed he would get over it in time. He didn't even bother to explain why he hadn't turned up this morning. *Good thing, anyway*, I thought miserably.

It was a silent meal on my part. I ate the food, not even noticing what it was, and escaped to my room as soon as I could, eager to be away from Mom and the strained looks of the Martins. It always seemed to me that Rev. Martin could see into my soul when he looked in my eyes. Not a happy thought even on my best days and especially not tonight.

I decided that whoever said that things are seldom what they seem was some kind of genius. I tossed around unable to sleep. Nigel was not a spy after all, but my mom was. Sort of. I still couldn't believe she worked undercover for a famous Nazi hunter. My mother, whom I thought I understood and trusted, had deceived me. I ached at being left out. How could she be something else, someone I didn't even know? When I closed my eyes, all I could see was her kneeling in that pool of blood, and I couldn't shut out the sounds of people crying and the smell of blood and smoke. She cared enough about them . . . strangers . . . that she nearly died.

And Hannah. Images of Hannah frightened by Herr Donner. Or Herr Donner out there alone and scared and running. Because of us.

I didn't want to think about any of that. But I couldn't stop and I couldn't sleep.

Voices from the front hall drifted into my room—sounds without words. *The Martins must be saying good-bye to Mom.*

I wished for the comforting sound of the train that used to put me to sleep, and then I remembered with a pang that Grossgmain was over for me. It would never be the same again. Nothing would ever be the same.

Although I couldn't hear his words, Pastor Martin's smooth, deep voice seeped into my brain like a benediction without comfort: *"Now unto Him that is able to keep you from falling, and to present you faultless before . . . the only wise God."*

But I was falling into a depression that blanketed me like the cold drizzle of the long, long day. I shut out their voices and fought the tears.

◆

The next morning Nigel was reading the paper when I stumbled sleepily into the kitchen.

"What's this? It's nine-thirty already. Why didn't you wake me up in time for school?" I asked. "And, Nigel, it's a little late for you, too, isn't it? Where's Mom? Hey, is my name in the paper?"

"Which one of those questions do you want me to answer?" Nigel asked dryly.

"The last one. It should say something like, 'Young man with a keen mind and brilliant memory helps the police capture terrorists,' right?"

Nigel smiled and handed me the paper. "Do you think your keen mind can handle reading this?"

Simon Wiesenthal was shot and seriously wounded yesterday. The gunmen apparently hoped to silence the famous Nazi hunter, whose research led to a recent series of successful indictments in German and Austrian courts.

Explosives destroyed much of Wiesenthal's office, which contained his extensive war-crimes research. Those injured in the blast include two unnamed male employees. Roberta Kaye, an American working for Wiesenthal, was also present but escaped serious injury.

No arrests have been made, but police believe the secret organization of SS officers once known as the Odessa carried out the attack. An eyewitness in the street provided information that may lead to the apprehension of the three men involved.

"That's it?" I asked, shocked. " 'An eyewitness in the street'? Fame is so fleeting. Mine didn't even survive the night."

I got up to put an English muffin in the toaster and pour myself a glass of orange juice. Last night's depression returned.

The stale smell of smoke lingered in the room. Ashes and cigarette butts lay in a dessert dish on the counter, reminders of the police convention in our kitchen last night.

"Use your head, Con," Nigel said. "Until these men are apprehended, it's a jolly good thing you aren't famous as an eyewitness. This isn't a game, you know."

"Yeah, I know. But I'm safe. 'An eyewitness in the street' is what I call a vague description—you know?"

"True. But he saw you when you saw him."

I remembered. Too well. "Is that why I'm home? To hide out?"

"Only partly. It was quite a day yesterday. We figured you needed the rest this morning." He added after a moment, "They could connect you to your Mom if they decided to watch her . . . and Hannah to you. There is some possibility of danger, yes."

I took my muffin to the table with the jar of Nutella, a European version of peanut butter. Nigel seemed to be waiting for my questions.

"So . . . you knew all along—about Mom working for Wiesenthal?" I asked, my bitterness coming through.

"Yes, I did. Before we were married, actually."

"I don't know why she didn't tell me. I thought I knew her. Better than anyone in the world."

"I think you do."

"We were always supposed to be honest with each other." Embarrassed, I remembered my deception of yesterday. "Honest about important things," I added.

"Honesty isn't really the issue, Con. I think you know that. And she did want to tell you."

"So why didn't she?"

He took his usual time. "Two reasons. First, we didn't feel you were ready to understand all the implications of what she was doing." He paused. "I mean this kindly, son, but your reactions now bear that out."

He waited, but I didn't feel like agreeing.

"And second, secrecy was vital for her safety and effectiveness. You would have been tempted to say something. However, for what it's worth, I felt you could have handled that."

"Thanks—I guess. It's too late now for secrecy. I mean with her name in the paper and all."

"Yes, I guess it is. She was able to go places and ask questions without putting people on the defensive, like she might have if she were Jewish."

"Did she know it was dangerous? Working for Wiesenthal?"

"A bit. But no—I don't think either one of us took it as seriously as we should have. Those men meant to kill Wiesenthal, and they certainly didn't care who got hurt in the process."

I shuddered at the memory of that scene. Mom's blood-stained shoes were still sitting in the front hallway. I could see them from the kitchen. My stomach hurt as I remembered the smell of the blood and my fear.

I pushed away the rest of my muffin.

"She could have been killed," I said. "How could she risk that? Didn't she think about me?"

Nigel didn't answer.

"Why her? That's what I want to know. I know awful things happened during the war. But it was over fifty years ago. And we're not even Jewish. It isn't her responsibility. Don't I matter more than some dead Jews? She wasted time and energy and took risks, even ruined a friend's life. For what? To be a hero?"

I went to the window and stared out, taking in familiar sights and sounds. The mailman was passing. I wondered if he knew how long it had been since this time yesterday.

"Did you know Gregor called yesterday? His parents don't want him to come around anymore. They think Mom's some kind of fanatic. I don't know, Nigel. Maybe they're right."

"I am sorry about Gregor, Con. I didn't know. Most Austrians don't like Wiesenthal or what he does. They would like to forget. However, I imagine Gregor's parents will change their minds in time."

"I don't care so much about that. Frau Müller has always been a little weird. Anybody that neat has to be weird. But even Dr. Reiks . . . he didn't say much, but I could tell he wasn't pleased, either."

Nigel came and stood beside me at the window.

"Your mother can—and will—explain her reasons, in her time. Allow me to give you a bit of advice, though. Do not try to understand and sort it all out at once. We can't do that when our feelings are involved. No one can. Give it some time."

"Time. How much time does Herr Donner have? He's a sick old man. This could kill him. Is that what they want?"

Again Nigel said nothing, and I blundered on. "Whatever

he did, he did as a soldier acting under orders. Like everyone else. Mom, Wiesenthal, Frau R.—all of them only want revenge." I was shouting now. "How can they?"

"Revenge could have been taken in other ways long ago. Justice, on the other hand, sometimes takes time," Nigel said slowly. "It is accomplished out in the open through the courts. The victims do not wish to become like their murderers."

"Revenge is just a part of justice then," I snapped. "Do the same thing, call it by another name."

We both stood at the window. Nigel was trying, I knew that. But his words didn't help, didn't change anything.

" 'Let justice roll down like a river,' " he said, more to himself than to me.

"What did you say?"

"Oh, I was just quoting the prophet Amos," he replied. "He said, 'But let justice roll on like a river, righteousness like a never-failing stream!' It appears God thinks justice is important and that we should help to bring it about."

I went on staring out the window, not seeing a thing.

"Con, eventually you will see. . . . It may not be for a long while, but you will be proud of her when you understand. She did what was right. And perhaps more important, she did it for the right reasons."

He reached over, squeezed my shoulder, then quietly left the room.

I heard Mom up and moving around, but I wasn't ready to see her yet. Feeling a little like a coward, I decided to go out.

Gone to the bakery. Be back shortly, I wrote on the notepad by the telephone and avoided, for a while, the inevitable talk with Mom.

10

REVELATIONS

BRANKO WAS SURPRISED TO SEE ME AND CALLED FRAU Loveric out front to watch the bakery while he walked me home.

"This seems a little melodramatic for Braungasse, don't you think?" I complained. "Those men were probably caught at some small border crossing last night."

"I don't know about that. I do know the police were quite specific. Besides, I thought you liked melodrama." He held the gate beside the stone post of our garden courtyard open for me.

"Branko, sometimes I do the dumbest things. They don't seem so bad at the time, but . . ."

He hesitated, then looked at me. He stood so straight—like someone at attention. His friendly eyes, as always, looked out of place in such a strong face.

"Like what?" he asked. He waited, unhurried, while I tried to figure out how to explain.

"Well," I began uneasily, "all that stuff about skipping school and Hannah being at our apartment when Herr Donner came . . . That was my dumb idea. I was looking for spies, and she was going to help me."

It sounded even worse out loud.

He chuckled. "You were, huh? Whom were you suspecting?"

He was not making this easy.

"Um . . . you and Nigel," I mumbled, kicking a stone with the toe of my sneaker. "Mostly Nigel. But, Branko, those men were so strange, and they were really angry. They didn't look like customers . . . and you seemed so mysterious about the judo and all that. I thought maybe that with the war in your old homeland, you might want to help out . . . and—"

"Hey," he stopped my rambling. "It was very much my fault for putting such ideas into your head. I wanted to cheer you up, and I knew the thought of intrigue going on around you would do that. I should have known you would want to take part in it."

Branko always had a way of making me feel better, and it worked again. But he still hadn't explained why he would want to keep his judo secret, and I figured now was as good a time as any to ask.

His answer was longer than I expected, and it surprised me.

"Con," he said, leaning on the gate, his expression intense as he explained, "I was always bigger than other boys in my class, and I was from a different country. Croatians didn't have such a good reputation after the war because many had sided with the Nazis, and I was teased. My brothers all fought back. Then and now. Then it was other schoolboys, now it's the Serbians.

"Because I was so large, the other boys expected me to fight, but I'm not a fighter. I took up judo as a defense, I think, to be able to defend myself. I still don't want to be seen as aggressive; I would rather people not know about the judo. It's that simple. And I've kept it up because I enjoy it and it keeps me fit."

"Boy, was I wrong!"

"Not so wrong as you think." He tipped the bill of my Redskins cap up and said, "Now, keep this under your hat."

I nodded.

"Those men who left in such a hurry—you were right about

them. They were not customers, and they were not nice men. Some people back in Yugoslavia think I should help continue our struggle against the Serbian invaders. There are things I could do living in Austria, intelligence I could gather for them, but I always say no. Those men you saw that day were sent to convince me otherwise. You did not imagine their anger, and you nearly got in their way. So you see, you were not so far off."

"Wow. That's cool, Branko. Thanks for telling me."

His response was quick and sharp.

"No, Con. It is not, as you say, 'cool.' It is dangerous. So no more games—you hear? The police said for you to stay out of sight for a few days until they know more about the men in the white Audi. You do as they say."

I didn't argue, not with an angry Branko. I watched him disappear up the street before I closed the gate and went inside, wondering why everyone was overreacting.

"Thank goodness you're back," Mom said as I came in the front door. "Nigel was just setting out to find you. The police said you shouldn't—"

"I know," I interrupted. "Branko told me."

Mom looked a little pale, but the trauma of yesterday was no longer so evident. She had come from the shower, her damp hair curled around her face, which was, as usual, without makeup. Neat little stitches held together the cut, surrounded now by small, purple bruises, evidence that yesterday was not a dream. We sat down at the sunny breakfast table. My half-eaten muffin was still there. I began to nibble on it nervously, still feeling uncomfortable with my own mother. She wore an old flannel shirt that hung loose over her jeans. Typical work clothes for her, but she looked different to me now sitting there with the sun on her hair, a sad, pensive look on her face. Waiting. Waiting to explain things I didn't want to hear.

The warm air blowing in the open window and the sun brightly lighting the room could not dispel the gloom between us.

"I'm off now, Roberta," Nigel said, coming into the kitchen to say good-bye. He kissed Mom on the top of her head and rubbed her shoulders. "I'll try to get back early. You two take care and try to stay out of trouble today."

As Nigel left for the office, Mom began to talk. She told me of her conversation with Sinnbrunner early this morning. Herr Wiesenthal was in stable condition, and no white Audis matching my description had been seen trying to cross at any border posts. At least, she added with some skepticism, none that had been reported.

"Herr Donner hasn't been seen, either," she said. "However, Frau Donner had a late-night visitor who arrived at about three A.M. by taxi. He helped her load up the Mercedes with an excessive amount of luggage and boxes, then drove her away from Grossgmain in it."

"Where would she go?" I wondered out loud.

"Well, they followed her to a farmhouse down near the Hungarian border. Frau Donner is still there, but there's no sign of Herr Donner. He could be underground right here in Vienna, of course—there's plenty of Nazi network still here."

"Don't you feel a little funny about being responsible for this?" I asked, my emotions heating up.

"Con, I'm sorry. I know this is upsetting for you."

"Upsetting? Upsetting for me?! What about the Donners? Run out of their home. Hiding. Facing arrest. I just don't know why you had to interfere. I mean, maybe he isn't what I thought he was. Maybe he did . . . I don't know . . . do things. But why couldn't you have left him alone? Why is it your business to ruin their lives? They are old people. And they were our friends—or have you forgotten?"

There was a long pause. Mom got up and refilled her coffee cup, moving like she was still sore. I finished off my now very cold, very hard muffin, chewing it with vigor. There was a small pile of spilled sugar on the table, and I started making roads in it with my finger.

Mom seemed unsure how to answer. *I'm right*, I thought, *and she knows it*. So I pressed my case.

"Where is the mezuzah now, Mom? I know you took it to Wiesenthal yesterday." I waited for her to deny it.

Ignoring my direct question, she said, "This isn't going to be easy, Con, for either of us. I have to tell you some things you won't want to hear, some of it you've already guessed." There was a pleading in her voice. The cold, calculating investigator of yesterday was replaced by the mom I knew, but I wasn't going to let her off that easy.

"What did you do with my mezuzah?" I asked again.

Her whole body stiffened. She sat up very straight, and the pleading was gone.

"I took it to Simon Wiesenthal's office and gave it to him for evidence to be used against Herr Donner in what will be his war-crimes trial. He will be charged with crimes against humanity, the legal term for mass murder." Her words were crisp, clear, and sharp—piercing. They stunned me—and she had meant them to.

"Good thing it was destroyed in his office then." I was still unable to stop myself from challenging her.

"But it wasn't destroyed," she answered. "And it is now in the safe custody of Sinnbrunner." There was a note of triumph in her voice.

"Sinnbrunner? What business is it of his?" I shouted.

"Evidence, that's what business it is of his. Last night after he left here, he went to the Documentation Center and picked up the entire file on Donner, which had been carefully placed in the safe just before those Nazi thugs arrived. I had completed my business and was in a hurry to get back to you when they broke down the door."

"Evidence of what?" I tried again. "Herr Donner told me he had only obeyed orders during the war, and I believe him. So he picked up some loot, Jewish even. Is that so terrible during a war? It doesn't prove he was a war criminal."

"Prove? Maybe not by itself. But along with all the other evidence, it proves a great deal indeed."

"Another nail in the coffin?" I asked bitterly.

"Yes, I hope so. Another nail in the coffin." Despite her words, her face had softened.

I groaned out loud. One day you live in someone's house, take the gifts he offers you, and the next day you're helping to put him in prison.

"Why him? Herr Eibel has all his Nazi medals—you saw them at the pension—but you aren't persecuting him. The guy who used to be president of this country was a Nazi and still lives in a big fancy house—you aren't bothering him. So why pick on an old friend? That's what I don't understand. Why set out to ruin him?" Tears welled up in anger and frustration. I wanted to hurt her, say something to make her feel hurt, too. Unable to win with words, I shoved back my chair and said, "I'm going outside. I don't care who is out there. It's safer than in here."

"Trust me, Con. Please trust me," Mom said softly, without the hard edge.

Something in her voice made me stop. I remembered Nigel's words, *"You will be proud of her when you understand."* Defeated, I sat back down.

"Forget what I did or why—I will explain that another time. For the moment let me tell you why the mezuzah he gave you is so important."

As her words rolled over me, I stared at the roads I had made in the sugar on the table. I knew I didn't want to hear what was coming.

"There was a message on the scroll inside the mezuzah. I saw it at once that morning in the apartment. It took me a while to read it all . . . exactly. But I knew immediately that Herr Donner had just handed us proof of his own war crimes.

"The mezuzah belonged to a boy just two years younger than you. He refers to the beautiful mezuzah as his new Bar

Mitzvah gift. The message was written in Hebrew, hidden in the text so no German eyes could read it. It was very cleverly done, not the work of a scholar but rather a bright young student. It took fifty years, but someone finally read his words last Saturday in Grossgmain.

"Raoul Levi of number 45 Grieskai, Graz, Austria, wrote his name and address and the name of his murderer. He knew no one would read his message in time to save him—he wrote in the past tense—so it was a plea for justice. He hoped, believed, that someday someone would know what had happened to him, to his community, to his family, and the man responsible would be punished. Like you, Con, he was clever and observant."

I was trying not to listen, but she went on.

" 'I watched everyone disappear,' Raoul wrote. And we know what he meant because it happened in Graz like it did in hundreds of other towns in Europe. People were rounded up and simply disappeared. He had watched evil come into his town and destroy his friends and relatives. One by one, the boys in his Hebrew class, their neighbors, the old women in black who sat in chairs beside the street gossiping—they all disappeared. He saw evil face-to-face; he knew the man's name, and he wrote it down."

Mom took a deep breath, then continued.

"Raoul went on to explain how the SS officer in Graz had a clever way of getting rich while doing his duty. First he would strip families of all their money and valuables, promising to protect them from deportation. And then he would return and carry them away with all the rest—no matter what they had paid."

I shivered even though the room was warm.

"We can only guess at some of the details, of course," Mom went on.

"But the boy recorded how the Nazi officer came to the Levi home and made his standard offer—'Your money or your life,' meaning to have both. Raoul's father, like the others, had no choice but to give the officer all they had—the treasures of generations of Levis—hoping at least to buy a little time for his family. Raoul had managed to hide his mezuzah, and while he waited with his family for the SS man to come back—because he knew he would be back—he wrote his message."

I felt myself shaking my head no, willing her to stop.

"The SS officer was one Commandant Helmut Donner, and Raoul dated his message by the Jewish calendar 7 Kislev, 5705, which was November 7, 1944. Exactly seven months before the Americans liberated Mauthausen, where the Jews of Graz were taken—where they died in the gas chambers made for them. Mauthausen, a small village in the beautiful Austrian countryside. Famous for its good farmland and efficient death camp."

She had stopped speaking, but the noise in my ears got louder—a terrible pounding like the sound of the train when it echoes in the valley. *Donner, Donner, Donner* kept screaming in my head. Over and over. Mom reached out and covered my hand with hers, increasing the pressure.

With her other hand Mom touched my chin, raising my face to look into hers. A red rash crept up her neck like streaks of fire against her white skin, and it was hard to understand her next words, they were spoken so softly.

"Son," Mom said lovingly. "Son. There is no connection between you, what you are, and a man who was once kind to you and what he is. You have to understand that before I go on."

I couldn't move; I couldn't shut it out.

"I'm going to tell you something now that may seem cruel. I am going to tell you because this very morning—now—you must cease to think of Herr Donner as some soldier who was obeying orders. Herr Donner was not a soldier. He was a murderer.

"You know how Donner always liked to play cowboy with you, Con, and hear stories about your grandpa the cattle rancher?"

I nodded, remembering how he had loved the real Stetson we had given him long ago. Mom put her hand back on mine.

"Well, it wasn't the first time he had played cowboy. It has long been known that the commandant of KL Graz liked to ride his horse racing through the crowded camp, shooting at random into the people. Children were often trampled to death, unable to escape the horse's hooves, or shot as targets in his game. But any mention of his name conveniently disappeared, lost when records were destroyed before the Russians arrived. . . . Lost, that is, until now."

I pulled away from her and stumbled to the open window, taking big gulps of air. "Stop," I said, unable to see through my tears. "Please stop, Mom. Don't do this to us."

Suddenly I knew it was true, even as I cried against it. And unable to stop them, images of Herr Donner in his fancy tooled boots, silver spurs, and hat, his big body lunging around the room pretending to shoot me, filled my head.

"Why didn't his evil show? Why didn't I see it? And why did you tell me? I don't want to know. I liked him . . . like him. . . . What's wrong with me?"

I ran from the room, from Mom's voice, from the truth she had just told me, and all I could see was that last scene in Grossgmain with Donner reaching into his pocket and bringing out more than he had meant to. *It's over*, I thought. *I know the worst, and it's over.*

What I didn't realize was that the present held its own evil.

11

STAKEOUT

It was two a.m. The words kept blurring on the page. I'm not a good reader at the best of times, and my mind refused to remain in ancient Greece and off the events of yesterday. After the emotion of the morning talk with Mom, my anger became restlessness. She hadn't said any more. She was, I knew, giving me some space—some time—but I was getting bored with "staying out of sight" and hated not even having Mom to talk to. Hannah had called in the afternoon; the police suggested she stay home from school, too, and not go out alone until . . . until what? I had asked. But she didn't seem to know. I thought her voice sounded a little cool on the phone. Maybe we were both uncomfortable. We didn't talk long.

Gregor never called.

So it had been a limbo kind of day. I wasn't allowed to go out at all. Occasionally a police car cruised past, maybe some unmarked ones, too, keeping an eye on us and looking for others who might be doing the same.

Life's funny, I thought. *Before yesterday, all this cop stuff would have been a thrill. Now . . . well, now it doesn't seem so exciting.*

Giving up on reading, I dropped the *Iliad* on my bed. *So much for homework,* I thought. *I could use some food.* I went into the kitchen for a late-night snack. Rye bread, peanut butter,

Cheez Whiz, and bologna. No self-respecting mother would limit her son to such a snack. But it was true—there was nothing else in our kitchen for a snack, and I didn't dare complain at two in the morning. So I put them all together and found that, when washed down with half a liter of Coke, it wasn't half bad.

I opened the kitchen window, and a cool, dry fall breeze blew in, silent as the night itself. No one moved on Braungasse after midnight.

Lost in my thoughts, the sound came close before I noticed it. Even then it took a moment to register. I heard the low hum of a very fine engine creeping up the street. Dried leaves crackled under its tires almost louder than the motor.

I was probably the only person on the whole street up at that hour, and I was sitting in front of an open window framed in bright light. A sitting duck.

I just saw the nose of the car as I dived to the floor. Feeling a complete fool, I crawled out of the lit kitchen into the darkened living room and up to the window ledge to peer over and see the car as it passed. But it had moved out of sight; I couldn't even tell if it was an Audi. Extremely glad no one had seen my mad behavior, and feeling a little sick from the rye bread, peanut butter, Cheez Whiz, and bologna sandwich, I went back to bed. Trying to laugh at myself for imagining Dirty Harry cruising Braungasse to gun me down, I went back to the *Iliad*, ready to be bored.

The light knock on my door a few minutes later was enough to make me jump again.

It was only Mom. She had heard a noise and came to check.

"Trouble sleeping?" she asked, taking a seat on the edge of my bed and picking up my book. "Maybe the *Iliad* is a little heavy for so late at night."

Mom looked as though she hadn't been sleeping much, either. We were quiet for a minute listening to the night sounds.

I was unable to stop myself from thinking about how Herr Donner had treated Hannah back in Grossgmain—the things

Mom said he had done. But the pictures in my mind of Herr Donner the cruel commandant were still blurred by Herr Donner my friend. And knowing that what Mom said was true didn't change the fact that I still wished she hadn't ruined the rest of his life.

We're not Jewish. They're not our people. Why couldn't Wiesenthal take care of it without my mom? I wondered.

As if she'd read my mind, Mom said, "Con, reach over there and hand me your Bible, will you?"

I wasn't in the mood for a sermon, but my resistance was low. My Bible was on my bedside stand among the disorder of school books, Asterix books, and notes I had made on my spy search. I pulled out the Bible. It was a nice leather-bound one Grandma and Grandpa Walker had given me when I was baptized and joined the church last year.

She opened it to Deuteronomy 6:4.

"Read it to me," she said.

" 'Hear, O Israel: The LORD our God, the LORD is one. Love the LORD your God with all your heart and with all your soul and with all your strength. These commandments that I give you today are to be upon your hearts. Impress them on your children. Talk about them when you sit at home and when you walk along the road, when you lie down and when you get up. Tie them as symbols on your hands and bind them on your foreheads. Write them on the doorframes of your houses and on your gates.' "

"Wait here," she said. Like I was going to get out of bed and go somewhere at this hour.

I heard her light footsteps run down the stairs in the hallway that led to her office and back up them again the same way. She had something in her hand when she sat back down.

I recognized it at once. It was a small, rolled-up paper that looked like the one from my mezuzah. She unrolled it and spread it on the pages of the Bible.

"I know," I said before she could tell me. "It's a mezuzah

text—like what was in my mezuzah. It's Jewish. So what? What does it have to do with us?" I was feeling very wary of the topic.

"Everything. It has everything to do with us." Her voice was insistent but not cross. "Jesus didn't do away with this commandment, Con. He took it one step further. Do you remember what He added?"

I hadn't gone to Sunday school my whole life for nothing.

"Sure," I said grudgingly. "Love your neighbor, too."

"Wrong," she said with a hard stare that always went right through me. "Not love your neighbor, too. Love your neighbor as much as you love yourself. Which is a lot in your case." She said that last bit with a smile. "I want you to think about this as you go to sleep tonight, Con. If Raoul and the other people of Graz had been your relatives . . . if one of the women tortured by Herr Donner had been your own grandmother, whom you love so much, or if Raoul had been your brother, then would you want to look the other way from what he and others like him did? If the skinheads of today threw stones through our window and beat me up, would you care? The answer is yes, yes, and yes. We do care about ourselves and our family. And it is impossible to love God without loving others equally."

She didn't give me a chance to respond.

"I'm still really tired, so I'm going back to bed now. You'd better get some sleep, too. You'll need it for tomorrow. Nigel has what I think will be a very nice surprise for you. For you and Hannah."

Despite my begging, she would say no more.

◆

The next time the door opened, sunlight poured through my window. I covered my head with a pillow and prayed that whoever it was would go away.

"I say, Con, you look a little green this morning," Nigel said, pulling off the pillow and dropping it playfully back on my face. "Not sick, I hope." His voice sounded terribly cheerful to my fuzzy brain. "I want you to go with me to Zürich today."

"What?" The pillow hit the floor.

"You and Hannah. It's all arranged with her parents. We're picking her up in one hour, so move your body to the shower and pack a few things . . . including books. You will have time to study while I'm working. Then we'll see a little of the city."

"Wow, Nigel! You're serious, aren't you?" I was wide awake now.

"I'm always serious. Do you think you two could stay out of trouble for a couple of days?"

"No problem! Hey, thanks, Nigel. I would ask why, but I don't want it to sound like I'm questioning your judgment."

He laughed. "Get ready."

After he left, I sat on my bed thinking. Nigel had never taken me on a business trip before, certainly not during school, so it didn't make sense unless the police were really worried about our safety. Cool. Who cared why? *Oh well*, I thought getting up. *I won't have to watch my back in Zürich.*

◆

"Are you sure you'll be fine?" Nigel asked Mom for the third time as we prepared to leave for the airport.

"M-hmm . . ." she murmured happily, settling down on the couch with a book. "Think of all the meals I won't have to make."

"Think of all your meals we won't have to eat," I said.

She threw her book at me.

Against Nigel's wishes, Mom was staying home. He tried one last time to convince her otherwise.

"You sure you won't change your mind and come with us?" he asked, picking up his briefcase. "It's not too late."

"No. I need some time alone to think. And I promise to be careful until you return. Branko is close by if I need anyone."

Nigel had reluctantly given in, and after picking up Hannah, we had to rush to make the plane. Rushing in the BMW was not a bad thing.

Hannah and I played cards on the plane, and we were so excited to be missing more school and going to Zürich that neither one of us mentioned Herr Donner—or any of that—during the flight.

I saw the lake, Zürichsee, as we banked to the left and flew over the city toward the airport. There were no boats dotting the water today. It looked like blue glass—quiet, cold, and not at all friendly.

Our hotel was right in the middle of old Zürich. Hannah and I spent Wednesday evening and Thursday morning enjoying the pleasures of a posh hotel and finishing most of our homework. I plodded through to the end of the *Iliad*, and together we finished a project for Ms. Gaul on Austria in the seventeenth century. We had studied Prince Eugene, who whipped the Turks and then retired to Vienna to build Belvedere Palace. Hannah and I had gone there to visit it for research and discovered fascinating things, like the croissant was made in honor of his victory, its crescent shape taken from the symbol of the Turkish empire. Our research had required sampling several different croissants, I recalled with pleasure.

By Thursday afternoon, though, we were besieging Nigel with all sorts of suggestions for seeing Zürich.

"What's to see in Zürich, anyway?" Hannah asked Nigel over dinner.

"Zürich's specialty cannot be seen by tourists, young or old," Nigel replied.

"Huh? You want to explain that, Nigel? 'Cause we don't buy that there's-nothing-to-see routine."

"I didn't say there wasn't anything to see, only that you can't see it." Nigel was obviously enjoying playing with us. "Zürich is famous for its hidden gold. Hidden, that is, in perfectly legal but numbered bank accounts to protect the identities of the holders. Everybody from rock stars hiding money from the tax man to dictators from around the world use the numbered bank accounts. It's a legal way to hide money. Lately they have gotten a lot of grief over the money that once belonged to Jewish victims of the Holocaust and is still safely stored in old Nazi accounts. Banking is what Zürich is famous for—not very exciting for the tourist, I'm afraid."

Absolutely refusing to go on any idiotic tours with elderly tourist types—or to believe Nigel's weak attempt to disinterest us in sight-seeing—the three of us finally agreed on his conditions. Which were ridiculous but accepted for lack of better ones. I still had the nagging suspicion everyone was trying to protect us. *Nigel must still be jumpy*, I concluded.

So the plan was this: We were to stay within a certain radius of the hotel—under no circumstances were we to go as far as the lake on our own. We were to meet him back at the hotel at four-thirty. Then we'd all go out for a cheese fondue together.

Not a thrill a minute. Still, it was better than the hotel. And the view was great from the narrow streets high above the lake. I bought a new Swiss army knife to replace the one I had left in Wyoming last summer. Hannah was as picky as ever and couldn't make up her mind, so she bought nothing.

The people of Zürich seemed as old as their city. Quiet and boring. We rarely saw anyone under the age of fifty, and after two hours of looking around, we were beginning to think Nigel had been right about nothing out there to see but banks. Not to mention Hannah was getting tired of my singing.

Then I saw it.

"That's it, Hannah! I can't believe it, but there it is."

"What?" she asked, looking around. "A blonde?"

"No, you idiot. The car. The same car." I approached the parked vehicle cautiously.

"The same car as what?" She looked at me like I was crazy.

"The same white Audi," I stammered with excitement.

"Come on, Con, get a life. It can't be the same car. Have you forgotten what city we're in?"

"I know it's crazy. . . . But it's the same car. Look at the scratch. It's exactly the same." I ran my hand along it, wondering if it was possible there was another white Audi Quattro with pale blue interior and the exact same scratch.

"Look at this," I said. "The scratch mark is identical. A perfect line from the front fender to the rear door. And on the same side."

"Then there must be a mad car-scratcher on the loose, with a nail hidden in his pocket, looking for white Audis. . . ." Despite her words, her voice trailed off and she had stopped laughing.

I walked around to the back and motioned Hannah to look. "See? The *D* sticker is in exactly the same place, centered over the license plate."

"But is it the same number on the plate?"

"No, it isn't," I admitted. "But professionals like those guys could, and probably would, change a plate before crossing a border, especially if they thought they had been seen. Remember the newspaper account said 'an eyewitness in the street.' "

"Maybe. But, Con, it isn't possible. We just happen to see the same car here in Zürich, Switzerland, on Friday that you saw Monday in Vienna?"

I knew it sounded weird. I also knew I had seen that car before, and I felt my first twinge of fear. "Stranger things have happened," I said.

"Yeah. Like Monday, come to think of it. Your mom turning out to be a spy."

"She isn't a spy," I snapped.

"Well, she isn't exactly Susie Homemaker, either."

"Listen, I'll prove to you and to the police that this is the same car. Those hit men are right here in Zürich."

"Sure you will. Want to tell me how?" She looked as skeptical as she sounded.

"You have your camera with you, don't you?" I said.

"Obviously." It was hanging around her neck.

"Well, we can stay out of the way, and when the men come back to get the car, we'll take their picture. I will definitely recognize Dirty Harry. I'm not so sure about the other guy, but so what?"

Hannah jumped away from the car, looking a little pale.

"Con . . . if it is their car—and I'm not saying that it is—but if it is, Dirty Harry will recognize you, too, especially if he sees you hanging all over his car."

I saw her point. We flattened ourselves in a nearby doorway. It turned out to be a watch shop. One of many.

"We can always go in here if they spot us taking their picture," I said nervously. It seemed safe enough. I knew it was the same car, but I would never be able to convince the police without some proof. So we settled in to wait. Hannah had her camera ready. She watched the street in one direction; I watched the other.

"You know, maybe we should go to the police," she said after a time.

"Oh sure. And they'd believe us? Besides, by the time we got a policeman here to look at the car, it could be gone. If we can get their picture and we have the new license plate number, the police might catch them."

She saw the logic in that and we waited.

Suddenly the door opened from the inside, and we fell into a quaint little watch shop. A small man in a dark gray sweater and with half glasses perched on top of his head held the door open for us and asked us not too kindly to stand somewhere else so as not to block his door.

"Sorry," said Hannah in English. "We were just coming in."

"Really? It took you long enough." His English was good and his manner a little less gruff now that he saw us as potential customers.

I continued to stand close to the door to watch the car. Hannah put on her best young lady voice and was doing a great job of keeping the little man hoping for a sale.

"So you want a watch for your mother. Did you have a specific watch in mind?" the shopkeeper asked.

I snorted under my breath. "Yeah, a free one."

Hannah gave me a dirty look.

The shopkeeper drew out two trays of beautiful women's watches. There were slim gold ones, large-faced modern ones, and delicately hand-painted bracelet ones that Hannah was getting genuinely interested in. However, she knew how much money she had in her pocket, and it wouldn't cover the tax on any of them.

Eventually the counter was covered with trays, and still Hannah didn't see exactly the right one. No sign of the men, either.

I sensed that our watch man was getting tired of the baloney and wanted to see some cash.

"Come on, Hannah, let's look somewhere else. You shouldn't make such a big decision without shopping around."

"You are so right," she said, heading for the door without any more prompting.

"I thought the Swiss were supposed to be friendly," I quipped as we left the shop and the withering glare of its owner.

"He didn't even say auf Wiedersehen. You would think he didn't want to see us again."

"Yeah, all we did was block his doorway for fifteen minutes, then waste thirty minutes of his time."

"I know," Hannah said. "And it shouldn't even take that long to put back all the watches I looked at. They were pretty. I really would like to buy my mom one."

"Sure, like you have the money, Hannah. But what the Swiss lack in friendliness they make up for in neatness. Did you notice how carefully he wiped the smudge marks from each watch you handled?"

We were walking slowly up and down the street, unable to

decide where to safely watch the car from without being seen or annoying someone else.

"I wish they weren't so neat," she said. "Where are we going to hide on this street? If this were New York City, we could just stay out of sight behind some bags of garbage or pretend to be homeless people or muggers—no one would notice. This whole country is as neat as Frau Müller's kitchen."

She had a point, and she also came up with the solution. Hannah's appetite came to our rescue as she spotted a sidewalk café up the street where we could wait and eat at the same time. I never could figure how she could consume so much food and stay so small.

"We don't have enough money," I said. "I spent most of mine on the Swiss army knife, and you never have any. Besides, it isn't close enough to take a picture."

"When we see them approaching the car, we could make a dash out of the café, then walk by pretending to be tourists casually taking pictures. Come on, Con, I'm starving."

"It might work. I could keep my head down so Harry won't recognize me. And it might be quite a while before they return to the car. I'm hungry, too. Let's go for it. Whatcha got for francs?"

Hannah dug around in the small leather pouch slung next to her camera. "I have enough for one Coke and one order of French fries. What do you have?"

I searched my pocket and came up with twenty-five francs.

"Oh great!" she said. "I'll just have to share my fries with you. You can at least buy your own Coke."

One hour, two Cokes, and one order of French fries later, we were getting bored waiting.

"Do you know," she said, "that when you eat at this speed, you actually get hungrier?"

I was looking at Hannah and had taken my eyes off the car. For a minute her mouth went on talking to me about food, but her eyes and attention had shifted to something down the street. Then her voice trailed off and finally stopped, like a battery-operated toy gone dead.

"Con, l-l-look. You were right—that guy does look like Dirty Harry. It's them."

My mouth went dry, and I froze to the chair.

"Come on, dummy—don't just sit there staring. We're going to miss them." Hannah was already on her way out of the café.

We had paid the check early so we could make a run for it, and I finally pried myself loose and did just that.

She was already moving up the street snapping pictures like a mad tourist.

"Don't run out of film," I muttered, catching up and trying to keep my head down and look at the same time. It was them all right. The two hit men and the same driver, who was fumbling with the keys while Harry and his much smaller accomplice waited, not too patiently, to open the doors on our side of the car.

My mouth was so dry I could hardly swallow. Hannah kept snapping pictures while I pulled my Redskins cap down a little lower and the collar of my leather jacket up.

We didn't mean to actually reach the car before they got in. Despite what seemed to be a snail's pace—to us—we were within hearing distance when a stream of foul German swear words, which I hoped Hannah with her limited German wouldn't recognize, erupted from the driver's side.

"Pick the blasted keys up," Harry growled at him.

The driver was having difficulty picking up the keys as he nervously tried to avoid being hit by oncoming cars on the very narrow, busy street.

Fascinated by the violent exchange, we did not slow our pace enough, and we came even with the car before they got in.

All three men were visibly and vocally angry. They continued to hurl abuse at each other as the driver finally managed to get the car unlocked.

Now I was having trouble breathing as well as swallowing. Hannah seemed cool and kept taking pictures. Dirty Harry hesitated, one hand on the back car door. I kept my face turned away and saw in the watch shop window his face reflected in the glass. Horrified, I realized too late that he was not getting into the car but standing stock-still watching me watch him. Both of our faces were mirrored side by side in the spotless glass.

I wished we hadn't been so stupid. And it had been very stupid to try to trick a professional killer. Then we made our second major mistake of the day. We ran.

Harry was a trained killer with split-second reflexes. It didn't take him long or very much effort to grab us both. Too frightened to speak, we struggled without hope of pulling out of his steel-like grip.

"What the. . . ? Stop him!" the driver shouted over the car, but it was too late. The third man had already slid into the front seat and couldn't react fast enough to stop our capture.

Harry shoved Hannah in first, against the far door. He kept hold of my wrist, twisting it up my back until I shouted in pain, but no one heard or noticed.

"You," he said to us over the startled outburst of protests from his companions, "are going for a ride with me."

"Fahren Sie," he shouted. "Schnell!"

The tires screeched as the driver pulled away into traffic and up the winding street as fast as traffic would allow.

"You," he said to us again, "are going for a long ride with me . . . to answer some questions."

It didn't look like we had much choice. The *thud* of the automatic door locks seemed to seal our fate.

WHO'S ON FIRST?

DIRTY HARRY, MY WORST NIGHTMARE, REACHED DOWN AND retrieved the Uzi from a case on the floorboard. *We're dead*, I thought, *and it's all my fault.*

I looked at Hannah—she was scared, but there was no sign of tears or panic. Fighting down my own panic and trying to think, I reached down to retrieve my cap, which had tumbled on top of the gun case when Harry shoved me into the car. I tried to give Hannah a reassuring smile. But it came out a little crooked as I winced in pain when Harry gave my arm a jerk, pulling me back against the seat without my cap.

If we had walked calmly on, common sense probably would have convinced our captor that he had been mistaken, that I just looked like the kid in Vienna. *Too late for what we should have done. What are we going to do now?* I wondered desperately.

The men continued to fight among themselves.

"Since you made the moronic move of kidnapping two tourists right in broad daylight from a Swiss street, you might have the brains to keep their heads down so only half of the good Swiss citizens will remember seeing them in our car," snarled a voice from the front seat. His voice carried authority. Dirty Harry obeyed.

He motioned our heads down with the Uzi, which he had been resting on his knee. It looked very deadly up close. We bent over, dropping our heads out of sight.

Evidently unable to speak clearly from anger and frustration, the same voice went on: "This had better be good, you idiot, kidnapping two kids right off the street in broad daylight in the middle of Zürich because one of them looks like the boy you saw in Vienna."

The driver demanded to know where they were going now: "The park to play with the kids, or take them to school?" He had a Low German accent and a stupid braying laugh that made him sound as well as look like a thug.

In the confusion and fighting among themselves, no one was asking us anything yet. It gave me time to think—I liked them yelling at each other instead of us.

Up close, Dirty Harry looked even more frightening than he had in Vienna. So far I hadn't heard his real name. His companions had called him many things but nothing his mother would have chosen. He continued to pressure my arm to the point of pain, giving it an extra push every few minutes for emphasis. I bit my lip to keep from crying out.

"Listen to me, Knut. I don't know how or why, but this kid"—he gave my arm another push—"was watching me now like he was in Vienna, before and after the hit. He saw my face both times. Astonishing, no?"

"No! Not astonishing. Insane!" Knut replied in a scream. "Totally insane."

Now I knew one name. I tried to see this Knut, who clearly seemed to be the boss. He had an upper-class accent and attitude. I could see his face glaring at me over the seat. It was contorted with rage, his neck swollen above his tie like it was going to burst. And he looked like he could cheerfully murder Harry.

"And that one." Harry ignored his remarks, reaching over and knocking Hannah's camera to the floor with his Uzi and kicking it with his boot. "That one took my picture when we walked up to the car. I couldn't exactly ask them questions there on the street. This"—he waved the Uzi at me again—"is the 'eyewitness' we have been worried about, right here in our car. Right where we want him." He twisted my arm again. "You'll be glad I took them, Knut . . . when I make them talk."

Knut didn't look convinced. My arm was killing me, and I was so scared it hurt.

"Oh, now I see." Knut's temper turned to sarcasm. "These are Wiesenthal's bodyguards, and they tailed us here to Switzerland on their bicycles." It wasn't meant to be funny, and only the driver laughed.

We pulled up to a major intersection, and the driver asked again, "Where to, boss, the zoo?"

"Shut up, Josef. You're paid to drive, not think or try to be funny," Harry lashed out at him. "There is a marina down by the lake that will be deserted this time of year. See if you can find your way there."

I could hear the sound of a map being unfolded. The fighting stopped as Josef and Knut consulted it about how to get down to Lake Zürich.

It was obvious that Knut carried some weight and that he thought our kidnapping was a mistake—not the first one that day, it seemed. They had already been arguing when we came upon them at the car. I figured they weren't too happy about Harry's failure to kill Wiesenthal, either. My grandpa's warnings to stay away from angry wild animals came to me then, and these men made Wyoming bears and rattlesnakes seem friendly by comparison. I could have used my grandpa's help, but I was thousands of miles from Wyoming. And out of reach of anyone's help. We were on our own.

Hannah's head was pushed up against the plush blue seat, her face turned away from me. My arm was hurting and Harry kept up the pressure. I shuddered to think what he might do to make us talk at the deserted marina. I preferred it the way it was, with everyone treating us as deaf mutes.

And then it came to me. One of my bright ideas, as Mom called them. Only this one had to work.

We had to convince these men that we were only American tourists unable to speak or understand a word of German. That would prove Knut's position and keep them divided and fighting each other . . . I hoped. *Only how can I warn Hannah before she blows it by saying something in German?* Even her very bad German would give us away.

Lucky for us, every time I had started to protest, Harry had shoved the gun in my side and said, "Shut up. You will talk when I tell you to talk." Fear had kept my mouth shut, and boy was I glad.

I didn't know how much of the angry exchange between the men Hannah had understood—enough to know we were in big trouble, I presumed.

Knut and Josef would be easy since they were already convinced we were just innocent tourists. Convincing Harry would be a different story. He had looked right into my eyes outside Wiesenthal's office. Going in and coming out. And I knew he knew when and where he had seen me before.

But there would be no way for him to prove I wasn't just another tourist, because my passport with its Vienna residence visa was safely back in the hotel.

"Oh," I groaned out loud, not from pain but from desperation. If Hannah had her passport in her purse, we were dead. Nigel had told us to take them when we went out today. I forgot mine, as usual, and I couldn't remember seeing the slim blue book in Hannah's leather bag when she was digging around for money in the café.

They were bound to search us—everything hinged on their not finding it.

It wasn't far from the old city to the lake. Rush hour was still a couple hours away, but traffic was heavy. I grew more and more convinced that my plan was our only chance. *If only Hannah—just this once—has been irresponsible and doesn't have her passport on her. If only I can warn her in time not to utter one word of German.*

It wasn't long before Josef brought the car to a stop by Lake Zürich. "You're here," he growled, still in a very foul mood.

I dared to look up a little and saw a grassy knoll with some trees and a couple picnic tables between them and a boat marina. The place looked depressingly deserted. It was too cold to sail, so the marina was closed for the season. What boats were there were moored for the winter with tarpaulins covering their decks.

Harry released my arm with a final shove and opened the door.

"Watch them," he ordered. "I want to check out that tool shed over there."

The other two men continued to angrily discuss the mess they were in, and I took my chance while they did.

"Pretend you can't speak any German," I whispered, hoping Hannah heard and they didn't.

"Shut up," Knut said in a tone that encouraged obedience. He was a violent and cornered man, and I didn't want to push him. But Hannah's face let me know that she had heard and understood.

I didn't think Knut wanted to add to their other problems by murdering two American tourists. Nigel would miss us at four-thirty and notify the police. We just had to convince Knut that his partner had made yet another mistake.

Harry came back and muttered, "Follow me."

They walked beside us—one on each side with Harry behind, his gun in my back—toward the lake and into the little tool shed. They pushed us down onto a pile of tarpaulins. Knut leaned against the wall opposite. Josef watched the door. Two small windows let in a little light.

Josef, now that I could get a good look at him, reminded me of other neo-Nazi skinheads—he just had a little more hair. But the look was the same: brutal, angry, and a little stupid in his case. I was feeling less confident of fooling him. He might torture for the fun of it.

I was counting on Knut to use reason. He was the boss, it seemed, and possibly the brains of the group. He had very white skin, dark eyebrows, and very little hair. Knut looked more like he would fit in on the Zürich streets. His conservative business suit made him look like a banker—not a nice banker, but I still thought he was our only hope for getting out of this.

Dirty Harry paced back and forth in that small space and began to question us—in German, of course.

"What did you think you were taking pictures of, anyway? Who are they for?" He got right in our faces, spitting out the words.

"We are tourists. American tourists," my voice cracked. Now that I was finally allowed to speak, I could hardly get out the words. But I knew *tourist* sounded the same in English and German and that he would get the idea.

"Speak German, you brat. Who are you?" Grabbing me by the shoulders, he shook me in frustration, eager to hit me but holding back. His breath smelled of beer, and he was even more scary up close.

"Let us go," Hannah pleaded, also in English. "Our parents will be worried."

We might have been pretending about the language, but the fear was real.

"Look, you." He turned to Hannah threateningly. "Shut up. I am not talking to you.

"I know you can speak German," he said, turning back to me. "And it is time you started. I saw you in Vienna on Monday, and you are no more a tourist than I am."

He pointed toward Josef and smiled. "Would you like my friend here to remind you how to speak German?" Josef looked eager to do so. He reminded me of the character in Gregor's video game. Torturing for fun.

My skin crawled, but I managed to look away from the menacing man and, in my best American accent, slowly enunciated "Not—from—Switzerland," as if I hadn't understood. "We're from Chicago." I figured he'd heard of it.

Harry grabbed my jacket and shoved me up against the wall. A nail jabbed me, but it didn't come through the leather. Despite the pain, I was encouraged by the fact that neither of the other two men stepped in speaking English. Harry obviously didn't know what to do next—bash us or keep trying.

After observing this for some time, Knut finally spoke up, his voice mocking. "Well, you have really done it now. They can't even speak German. Most American tourists can't, you know. So you kidnap two kids—a girl even—because they take your picture and one of them looks like a boy you saw at the hit. I am sick of you and sick of this job. Nothing has gone right. You couldn't even kill Wiesenthal. A helpless old man sitting still at his desk. Kids and old men. You can't take care of either."

That was too much. Harry turned me loose and lunged toward Knut, threatening to kill him. I thought for a moment he was going to try. But something held him back, and Harry turned his rage on me, spitting in my face as he yelled, "I'm trained to see things, and I tell you I saw this boy in Vienna." He poked me with the gun. "I don't know who the girl is, but she looks like a Jew."

As if she were an exhibit, he pulled Hannah up in front of them. "See? A Jew. A miserable little Jew. Maybe even Israeli. And we could take care of her right here, right now."

There was loathing on all their faces. My heart sank as I realized they were considering the suggestion. *Oh, God, please, please,* I cried silently. *Don't let them hurt her!* I was tempted to scream at them. I knew a few choice words in German myself. But I kept quiet. I got her into this, and somehow I had to help her get away.

Reason overcame desire and took control in Knut. He turned back to his partner, pointed at me, and said, "And him? Look at his blond hair and blue eyes. You going to kill him, too?" He went on with his voice rising. "We are not going to kill two American tourists. Even the Jewish one—we can't afford the heat. No more foul-ups! Clear? We mess this up and we are out—out of the organization, out of the party. Jörg, our great leader, does not like failure."

I looked at Hannah. She looked more sad than afraid. There was something there I couldn't read, and I felt distant from her for the first time since they had grabbed us. It was like a racial line had been drawn, and she knew she was on the other side from me. When I looked at those three men, I saw only Donner's face, and it was smiling at me, like he always did. I realized then that Donner was really just like these men. I remembered how he had looked at Hannah like that, too. I hated him for making me one of them.

Knut was still speaking, only now in a very controlled, businesslike voice. "Whoever they are, the cops are going to be all over this thing by morning. We better make sure no bodies are found before noon tomorrow. Dead or alive. We can still pick up our money at the bank as planned as soon as it opens. These two"—he motioned at us like we were rubbish—"haven't understood a word we've said, so we store them and get out of this country before they are found."

Josef, who had brought Hannah's camera from the car, flicked it open and ripped out the film, exposing it to the light. He tossed her beautiful camera in the dust at her feet. "Ja. I think Knut's right. No way some kid could've been at the hit watching you and then tailed you here. Let's dump these American tourists—she won't be taking any more pictures—get our money, and get out of this country."

"Shut up, Josef. Just shut your mouth." Harry turned the gun on him.

Knut moved between the two men. "We don't have time for this. Question them in English. Let's see what they do know. You do speak English, don't you?"

"A little," Harry said.

My heart nearly stopped.

"But yours is probably better. You do it."

"Not me," Knut said. "I never bothered to learn the filthy language."

Just as I was about to think we'd made it, Harry did what I was afraid of—he started looking for passports. He started with me and found nothing. I held my breath while he searched Hannah.

"Passport, passport," he shouted at her. "Give me your passport."

I couldn't breathe.

"My passport's in the hotel," Hannah said in English.

Yessss! I wanted to jump for joy. *We are going to make it.* None of them could speak English. I was sure of it. Especially when Harry started questioning us in his "little English."

"You who?" he asked, proud of his English.

"Who's on first," I said back without thinking. It just sort of popped into my head.

"You who?" he said again.

"No, you-who is on first."

"First? What first?" He threw up his arms in frustration, already having used up his little English.

"What is on second, you-who is on first," I said patiently.

Harry looked confused. He seemed less dangerous standing there speaking broken English. I should have known better than to get carried away. I couldn't help it, though; he walked right into it.

"Who—what—you who?" He raised his voice in frustration.

"No, I am not. You-who is on first. What is on second."

He looked to the other two for help. "I no know. I no know," Harry said. The other two shook their heads, enjoying his humiliation.

"I no know. You who?" he tried once more.

"I-no-know is on third; it is you-who on first," I replied helpfully.

With a straight face Hannah said, "Con, I don't think he

understands American baseball."

That did it. Harry swung the Uzi around and hit her full in the face, knocking her over. Blood spurted out on Harry as Hannah fell face down in the sawdust, turning it red.

"I told you to shut up, you Jewish pest."

In German Harry was very menacing, and I wished I hadn't provoked him.

I kneeled beside her to see how badly she'd been hurt. "I'm sorry, Hannah. Are you all right?"

She was moaning and the blood was still pouring out, but she managed a "Yeah, Con."

Knut stepped in before Harry hit me, too.

"That's it. It's over. Enough," he thundered at Harry. "Like I said, we don't want some busybody stopping in to check on their screams. Admit it. You kidnapped two kids—not Interpol agents, not Wiesenthal's bodyguards. You blew it, and now you are getting us out of it. Hide them where they won't be found before noon tomorrow. And do it now."

He pushed Josef aside, yanked the door open, and turned back to Harry. "Now," he screamed. "Right now."

It's a good thing looks can't kill, because Dirty Harry knew I was lying. Fortunately for us, he couldn't prove it. And Knut was obviously the boss. He continued to stare at me as he told Josef to go and find a place on one of the boats to hide us.

Josef left, and the other two found some rope in the shed and tied our hands behind our backs. Tight. As they pushed us out into the daylight, I looked at Hannah's face. It was still bleeding, blood running down her face into her mouth.

I avoided her eyes. This was my fault. *Me and my stupid ideas and smart mouth.*

The sun was getting low in the sky as the men hurried us toward a small yacht where Josef was standing. I looked around desperately, but the whole area was deserted. Even the water looked cold and lonely.

One corner of the tarpaulin had been pulled loose, and Knut

shoved us down into the cabin underneath it. The lapping noise of the water against the boat was our only welcome. I thought of Nigel; he and I had sailed together a few times. I wondered if he would ever find us here, even if they left us alive.

Harry threw us onto a bunk, and Josef helped him tie our feet.

"Not so tight," I said, catching myself in the nick of time from saying it in German.

Unable to resist any longer, Harry hit me and sent me sprawling onto the floor. With my hands and feet tied, I landed on my face without protection and a splinter slid up my cheek, burning like fire. I cried out in pain.

He laughed. "That's for Vienna. The rest comes later."

"Con, Con," Hannah gasped. "Are you all right?"

When she spoke, Harry pulled her right up to his face and said, "Listen, little Jew, I think you understand me just fine. So you understand this. There is nothing I would like better than to shut you up for good. So make one more sound and I'll send you where we sent the rest of your relatives."

It was his laugh as he spoke that did it. I saw Donner shooting babies for sport, playing the cowboy. And I heard his laugh as he had played with me. Harry and Donner merged together as one in my head. I knew that what they were doing was wrong, and I knew what I had to do.

"I am Jewish, too, you Nazi piece of dirt. I'm Jewish, too."

The problem was, I said it in perfect German. I mumbled it in the floor where my face was still planted. But I said it—in German.

Harry was still holding Hannah up by her jacket when he heard me. He dropped her—literally—onto the floor and shouted, "Did you hear that? The kid just said something in German. I told you he could speak German. Josef, get Knut back in here."

"Keep your voice down," Knut said, poking his head back in the cabin. Hannah was looking at me in utter amazement, not anger, not even fear. I couldn't believe I had done it, either, but I wasn't sorry. In fact, there was a great deal more I wanted to say to them in their mother tongue. Fortunately for us, I wasn't given the opportunity. Harry was explaining excitedly that I had just proved his point. He looked at Josef.

"I heard something. I don't know that it was German. Sounded more like moaning to me," Josef mumbled.

"You are too dumb to recognize your own language, you miserable weasel." Harry shoved him aside, appealing to Knut one last time: "The kid said, 'Ich bin Jude.' The kid spoke German!"

At that Knut knew his partner had gone crazy. The last thing in the world I would say, in any language, if I had understood anything at all, was that I was Jewish—and Knut knew it.

In a voice full of rank and authority, he said, "Gag them. Throw them in the head and get back to the car by the time I do. And I'm not going to walk slow."

He left. The other two did as they were told—quickly. But as Harry closed the door of that tiny, cold toilet, he whispered to me, "I will be back. Alone. And before you die you will tell me who you are and why you are here. I promise you that, boy."

Then he was gone and there was total darkness. Only his hate remained—and his promise. And I believed him. We felt the boat rock as they stepped off. We were alone. How long would it take him to get back?

The boat's head wasn't any bigger than our bathroom in Grossgmain. With our backs against the wall, knees doubled up and feet pushed against the toilet stool, we filled up the entire space.

When they shut the door, the darkness was absolute, the air cold and stale.

Hannah was rubbing her gag on the toilet paper holder, and without much effort, she slid it off. Then with her teeth she untied mine. I guess they didn't really expect anyone to hear us in there anyway or they would have done a better job. But we didn't yell for help for fear they would return.

The ropes were not so easy. We were not supposed to get out of them. So after a while we stopped struggling and tried to think. At least we could talk without being hit.

"Your face hurt much, Con?" she asked.

"Not as much as my hands and feet. The ropes are so tight. How about you? Your face looks pretty awful."

"Thanks."

I was comforted. I figured she was okay if she could still be sarcastic.

"Um . . . I guess I got you into trouble again, Hannah. I'm really sorry. But I'm sure Nigel and the police will find us." I didn't feel as optimistic as I sounded.

"I don't know why they should. This isn't exactly a public john."

"Maybe not. But don't underestimate Nigel. I've been doing that, I think. Anyway, he will miss us and get the police on it. Maybe someone saw the car down here by the lake. Maybe our watch man saw them take us."

We were quiet for a while, testing our ropes, trying to get relief. I had the irrational fear that we were using up all our oxygen.

Talking was easier than thinking. So we talked. About things we usually would have avoided. I ended up telling her all about the mezuzah and Raoul's message . . . and my anger at what Mom had done and now how ashamed I felt of those feelings. I was glad it was dark. I talked for a long time. Hannah was very quiet when I finally stopped talking.

In a very small voice she said, "Is that why you said that about being Jewish? Risked everything just to . . . stand with me? I'll never forget that, Con." I heard tears in her voice.

"Well . . ." Unable to explain and touched but uncomfortable by the emotion, I said lightly, "We do worship the same God, you know."

"Uh-huh—but we aren't both Jewish, and that wasn't a

very healthy time to convert. You almost got us killed with that choice bit of German."

"Right then I didn't care. I couldn't believe they hated you like that."

"Harry wasn't exactly crazy about you, either."

"No," I agreed. "But he had a reason. I did see him in Vienna and he knew it. Knows it." I shuddered at the thought, then added, "He wasn't too crazy about the Abbott and Costello routine, either."

It broke the tension, and despite everything, we both laughed thinking about it.

After that there was silence for a time while we both moved a little trying to ease the pain, but nothing helped. The knots were tight, meant not only to hold but to hurt. Every muscle screamed to move. My fingers were completely numb but throbbing.

Leaning forward to take some weight off my legs, I pushed against the head and felt the pressure of my knife box pressing against my chest.

"My knife!" I yelled into the cold and dark. "Do you hear me? The knife I bought earlier today . . ."

"Stop yelling, you idiot. Of course I can hear you. Why didn't you think of it sooner? Can we get it?"

We were both talking at once. It hurt us to move, but it didn't matter now. We had a chance.

"Let's get it. Let's get out of here. Hurry before Harry comes back," Hannah said, voicing for the first time my fears.

"Okay, okay . . . calm down. We have to think, figure out how to do this," I said, not feeling calm at all. "It's on the inside pocket of my flight jacket. The leather is thick, so that's probably why they didn't notice it when they looked for my passport." *Oh, Grandma*, I thought, *thank you for this jacket. It has saved my life.*

"My teeth are the only thing I have free," Hannah said. "Let me try to reach it that way."

We practiced turning so that she could drop it into my hands. I would open the box, take it out, and cut Hannah's ropes.

Our movements were clumsy and painful, but we were within reach of freedom—so close we could taste it.

I took a deep breath and prayed.

"Now," I said.

Hannah twisted as far as she could and pulled it out on the first attempt. I could feel her body quivering from the strain as she moved carefully, leaning behind my back.

"Careful," I said. "Hold on tight till you are sure. . . . Get as close as you can . . . you're almost there. . . ."

Thud. I felt it drop safely into my hands.

"I've got it, Hannah. I've got it." It was working. The boat rocked a little with a wave, and I felt sick with nerves. What if that was Harry, returning now that we were almost free? I had to get the box open, but my fingers felt totally numb.

"Be careful, Con—don't hurry, do it slow."

I was trying desperately to open the box. I had broken the seal when I had taken it out and looked at it earlier. *So it should open*, I thought. Finally I felt it give and the knife dropped out. Right out of my swollen, stiff fingers and onto the floor. With another gentle rocking of the boat, it slid into a little groove in front of the toilet. Totally out of reach.

13

LET JUSTICE ROLL DOWN

HOURS AND HOURS PASSED. I THINK WE SLEPT OFF AND ON, only to wake in the total darkness of that cramped cabin. The Swiss night had turned very cold, and that added to the pain in our aching limbs. Occasionally we shouted, but we didn't really expect it to do any good.

Each time a wave rocked the boat, I thought it was Dirty Harry back to make good on his promise.

"He's not coming, Con," Hannah said miserably. "But neither is Nigel. And maybe before it's over we will wish old Harry would come back and finish us off. 'Cause we're not gonna get out of here."

I felt the same way. The pain was terrible . . . but it was my thirst that made each minute more unbearable than the one before it. The blackness of that hole had swallowed up our spirits—real desperation had set in after I dropped the knife. Hannah didn't say so, but I knew that not only had I gotten us into this, but I had also blown our only chance of getting out when I dropped the knife. I was amazed at my feelings. I had failed her—brought her into this, let those men hurt her, and then failed to save her. She had never whined or complained. *Oh, Hannah*, I thought but couldn't say it, *I'm so sorry*.

Then it came. It was definitely a footstep, not just a wave that rocked the boat this time, and we both felt it. Something or someone had stepped onto the boat.

Panic now overcame my pain, my thirst, everything else. The thought of facing Harry without the others to hold him back was so shattering that at first the voice calling my name didn't even register—I couldn't even speak.

Hannah was quicker. "We're here . . . in here. . . . Help! . . . Help!"

"Con? Hannah? Is that you? Where are you?" Nigel called, scrambling toward our voices.

It was a small boat, and it didn't take him long to find us. He nearly pulled the door off getting to us.

"Con, Hannah . . . thank God you're safe." He was already gently lifting Hannah out of that hole, comforting her as he did so.

"I told you he would come, Hannah. My dad found us." I felt my voice trembling. "My dad found us," I repeated to my-self, tears of relief and joy stinging my eyes.

"These legs won't hold up anything," said a hefty Swiss gendarme helping Nigel get me out. "Just relax, boy, and let us help you."

Which I did, gratefully.

Everything was a blur for some time after that. The smell of the water and a reddish glow of early morning light greeted us. A new day—I hadn't been sure I would ever see another one.

They cut off our ropes on the deck of the boat with police swarming all around. "The pain is going to get worse before it gets better," the gendarme told us. "And," he added with fierceness, "I am going to enjoy catching the slime who did this to you."

We were carried on stretchers to an ambulance that was backed up to the dock, its siren screaming and lights flashing. Nigel climbed in after us.

The circulation began to return to our limbs and with it the pain—as promised.

As I lay there wrapped in blankets alongside Hannah,

Nigel's face looked haggard and worried. The usually starched white shirt and perfectly pressed suit were wrinkled and limp. Nigel said very little as we drove away from the marina. The muscles around his bloodshot eyes were tense as he firmly but gently rubbed our fingers and toes, now throbbing with pain as blood began to flow once again.

"How'd you find us?" I managed to ask through the muscle spasms.

Before he could answer, Hannah added, "They were coming back, Nigel. One of them, the one Con called Dirty Harry, promised he would come back. And he would have killed us. . . ." She was crying now after it was all over.

"I know," he said. "I know. But we got there first—it's okay now." Nigel's snow-white starched handkerchief became red as he wiped away her tears, which flowed through dried blood.

"Hannah never let those creeps see her cry. . . . She was so tough," I weakly tried to explain how incredibly brave Hannah had been.

"Shh, rest, both of you." Nigel ran his finger along the long, deep splinter in my cheek, wincing as he did so as if the pain were his own, and he muttered promises that those men would pay for what they had done to his son.

Painkillers, relief, and exhaustion finally kicked in, and the last thing I remembered for some time was Nigel's words. I liked the way he said "son," and I wondered through the fuzziness of my brain how on earth he had known Harry was coming back.

Examined, treated, sewn up, and released, we arrived back at the police headquarters for detailed questioning. While Nigel had filled us in on much of what had happened while we were at the hospital, there were still many things we both wanted to know.

The information we had given the police on the boat confirmed for them what Nigel had already convinced them of. It simply added new information to the city-wide manhunt that was already underway, thanks to Nigel.

Stiff but now able to move without much pain, we walked into the office of Chief Inspector André Schwarz, whom we had first seen with Nigel when he opened the door to our prison.

"Well, you were right, Mr. Kaye," the inspector said after exclaiming how much better we looked than when he had last seen us only hours before. "And I am very glad we listened to you." He went on greeting Nigel warmly, pumping his hand up and down. "And I don't mind saying, I thought you were a bit unrealistic at first."

Inspector Schwarz turned to us. "You have him, not the Zürich police, to thank for your safety. This man was a hero last night."

Nigel looked embarrassed and tried to change the subject. "Have you found anything yet? Any sign of them?" he asked.

"All in good time," Schwarz assured us and proceeded with his praise for Nigel.

Like the rest of Switzerland, his office was neat and orderly. A large window overlooked a courtyard filled with neat white Porsches, each with broad, red stripes running along each side and a bright red light perched on top. "Imagine a country with Porsche police cars!" I had exclaimed to Nigel when we arrived Wednesday afternoon. In the distance I could see the Alps.

Two mugs of piping hot Swiss chocolate sat on an otherwise bare desk.

"Please," he said, motioning to them. "For you." We settled back to drink the rich, creamy chocolate.

Hannah, who couldn't stop shivering, was wrapped in a blanket with *Polizei der Stadt Zürich* in red letters across it. Her stitches were covered with a white square patch that disappeared behind her hair, which fell over it when she tipped her head to drink. Deep, dark circles like half-moons ran underneath her eyes. The friendly policewoman who brought the hot chocolate patted Hannah on the back, gave a tuck to the blanket, and assured us she was at our service.

Nigel leaned back in a chair that was too small for his frame. He looked too weary to stay awake. He had refused an offer to rest and listened as Schwarz repeated the events of yesterday evening.

"When you two kids didn't return to the hotel by five o'clock, Herr Kaye became worried," the inspector began. "At five-thirty he was very worried. At six he was going door to door in the area of the hotel. And at twenty past, with ten minutes before all shops closed, he happened to walk into the shop of your friendly watch dealer. You two had certainly made an impression."

Hannah grinned at the memory.

The chief inspector didn't seem to be in any hurry. He was enjoying the story. "So Mr. Kaye brought the poor man here, right then, to describe what he had seen. And he insisted on seeing me. No one else. 'Whoever is in charge and can make decisions quickly.' I think that is how you put it, Herr Kaye."

Nigel shrugged, continuing to look a little embarrassed.

"As it turned out, the watch dealer had seen quite a lot. Enough to make him worry. When you two came strolling back, he was still a little cross about his wasted time showing the young lady watches. He saw the scuffle and felt that something was not right, but he convinced himself the two of you were probably playing around again and didn't report anything."

The inspector was interrupted by a phone call. We heard his side, which was short: "Everyone is in position. Everything is ready. Good, I'm standing by."

Without missing a beat he went right back to his narrative.

"The watch dealer did not remember if the car was an Audi or not. He obviously doesn't have your eye for cars," he said to me with a wink. "But here was the thing that convinced your father: The car was white.

"At Herr Kaye's insistence—" Schwarz turned in his swivel

chair to look out the window for a moment before continuing—
"I called the Vienna police and talked to a Detective Sinnbrun-ner. Then I began to believe it might possibly be the same men wanted in Vienna and that they had recognized you. We put out a city-wide search at one A.M. How do you say in America . . . all-points bulletin? It covered trains, planes, and border cross-ings."

The chief inspector was having a good time telling us this story, but his voice became serious when he said, "This Detec-tive Sinnbrunner in Vienna didn't seem to think your chances were too good if Herr Kaye's theory was right—that the ter-rorists were here to receive money for their Vienna job from a Swiss bank account and you had accidentally stumbled onto them. He was very impressed with you, young man, and was very relieved to hear we had found you unharmed."

"Unharmed?" Nigel protested. "I would say they did great harm to the kids. And," he said, turning to me, " 'accidentally stumbled onto them' isn't quite accurate—is it, Con?"

I gulped as the inspector leaned over his desk and asked us very directly, "Exactly what on earth made you two do such a thing, anyway? Hanging around the terrorists' car like that . . . what were you thinking?" He shook his head in utter amaze-ment.

"Um . . . could we please have more hot chocolate?" Han-nah asked, sparing me from answering that question.

Nigel laughed.

"But I still don't understand how the police found the boat," I insisted, rubbing my fingers together to stop them itching. They looked like overstuffed German sausages—crack-ing at the seams—but at least the horrible throbbing pain was gone.

"Well," Nigel explained this time, "after hours of waiting, we finally got a call that a patrol car was following a white Audi that fit the description perfectly. One occupant.

"They gave chase, only they got too close and the Audi lost

them, very professionally I'm afraid, but not before an identification was made. It was Dirty Harry all right."

Schwarz took over the story again. "We like Clint Eastwood, too," he said. "It was at that point that you"—he pointed to Nigel—"insisted we search everything in the direction that car was pointing when spotted. It was our only lead and only hope."

"But how did you find us in the boat, Nigel?"

He stood up and paced around the room. "The chief inspector was kind enough to let me go with him when he joined the search," Nigel said.

"I don't remember I had a choice," Schwarz chuckled. "But I'm a parent; I understood his worry. We went together. And as we were heading toward the lake, the empty marina seemed like a good place to hide a couple of kids. And the rest you know."

"I am grateful, really," Nigel said. "You were very patient with me, and it was excellent police work finding the kids so quickly." Nigel still paced. "But now those thugs must be caught. The banks close soon. If they are going to attempt to retrieve their money, it will have to be in the next hour. What is keeping them?"

I looked at Hannah to see if she was thinking what I was thinking. Harry had been on his way to finish us off when the police spotted him. If Nigel hadn't forced things, Harry would certainly have kept his promise. Despite the warm office and stomach full of hot chocolate, I shivered. Hannah pulled the blanket around herself and met my eyes. She was thinking the same thing: Harry, Knut, and Josef were still out there on the loose. Would they leave Zürich without their money or take a chance on getting caught when they showed up at a bank this morning?

Inspector Schwarz spoke again. "The tool shed seemed a likely spot—we saw blood in the sawdust and found your open and smashed camera, Hannah, which made us dead certain the two of you were nearby. From there a search of the boats."

"From there to our boat." I looked at Nigel and said to Hannah with an attempt to be my usual cocky self, "I told you he would find us . . . a piece of cake."

TOP SECRET

14

RETURN TO BRAUNGASSE

THE PRESS HAD AGREED, AT THE CHIEF INSPECTOR'S REQUEST, to keep a lid on this whole story until the trap set for the terrorists could be sprung. Kidnapping American kids was definitely news, and TV cameras were in the police station waiting for the action.

We were waiting, too. Inspector Schwarz seemed to be a patient man now that everything was ready, and he showed no stress. However, catching the terrorists before they left Switzerland was very important to him professionally. And for some reason it was important to him personally. I remembered the look on his face as he cut off our ropes. He hadn't looked so kindly then.

"See this point?" He took a small compass from his desk drawer, laid a city map on the smooth oak surface, and said, "That is where you kids spotted the car. From what you overheard of their conversations, it appears the three of them were returning to their car after attempting to withdraw cash when you, shall we say, ran into each other. Now they must return to the same bank today to complete the transaction. Unfortunately, what they failed to mention in front of you was which bank. Too bad. Nevertheless, thanks to your command of the German language—which is going to be a nasty surprise to them—we do know enough."

He turned the compass and drew a large circle around that spot. "That is a one-mile radius. Every bank in here"—he pointed at several locations with his pen—"has more police than tellers. It is highly unlikely the terrorists would have walked even a mile from where they parked. But we are not taking any chances. Now it's up to them."

"They'll all show up," I said. "I don't think Harry will tell Knut about being spotted last night. He wouldn't want to admit another mistake, and they all seemed determined to get their money before leaving." Maybe it was wishful thinking, but the idea of Harry remaining free was too terrible to think about.

"Hope you're right," Nigel said and Schwarz agreed.

"We'll know soon."

Our job was to wait at the station and identify the three when they were brought in. The problem was I wasn't sure I was ready to face Harry again even in the safety of the police station. But that fear was mixed with the happy prospect of greeting him in perfect German.

Lunch arrived, and we watched the clock while we ate the crunchy hard rolls, ham, and good Swiss cheese. But tension built in me at the thought of seeing him again, and I lost my appetite.

I found myself running my finger over the soreness on my cheek where the sliver had been. I was going to keep that piece of the boat forever. It was carefully wrapped and in my jacket pocket with the knife the police had found and brought back to me. Nigel began to pace restlessly around the room, not eating, looking at his watch. Inspector Schwarz left the room periodically.

"Do you know, I think I would have preferred Ms. Gaul's class over this trip to Zürich, Con," Hannah said to take our minds off the clock.

It took only a second to think that one through.

"Nah," we said together, laughing nervously.

A triumphant-looking officer motioned his chief outside the

room. Schwarz returned with a smile on his face.

The perfectly timed Swiss clocks chimed one o'clock as Dirty Harry and gang were brought in under heavy guard. Unaware of what was about to greet them, they still had the defiant look of professionals.

My heart skipped several beats. But when they got close enough, I greeted Harry as planned, in perfect German: "Done any sailing lately?"

"I knew it. . . . I knew it was you. . . ." He lunged at me, his face contorted with rage. It took several men to wrestle him down as he continued to hurl verbal abuse. "They heard every word we said, you ignorant louts." He turned on Knut and Josef, as eager, it seemed, to tear them apart as me. "That's why the police were waiting for us. . . . I told you," he went on ranting.

Knut was still wearing a business suit, but robbed of the money he had almost gotten his hands on in the local Kreditanstalt and finally aware that Harry had been right about us, he looked more murderous than the other two put together.

"That man," I said in German, pointing to Harry, "is the man I saw with the gun coming out of the building in Vienna, and he is the one who picked us up yesterday afternoon and threatened to kill us. He"—I pointed to Knut—"goes by the first name of Knut and seems to be the one in charge. He was the other man who came out of number 7 Seitenstettengasse after the hit. And that man, Josef, was driving both times."

Remembering how they had looked with such loathing at Hannah made this moment very sweet indeed.

Hannah nodded to confirm my identification but was unable to speak.

◆

Dirty Harry turned out to be Hans Grunwald. That was the name they booked him under. But he would always seem like

Dirty Harry to me. A man whose path I sincerely hoped would never cross mine again.

On the way to the airport, Nigel directed the taxi driver to stop at our friendly watch shop to buy Mom a Swiss watch and say thank you to the man whose memory had helped save our lives.

Hannah borrowed money from Nigel to get one for her mom, too. After all I had gotten her into in the past week, I decided not to tell Nigel what a bad credit risk she is.

It was Saturday afternoon before we arrived back at Schwechat Airport in Vienna. The BMW that Nigel had left at the Vienna airport was waiting. Hannah stretched out in the backseat with a book over her face. Nigel seemed lost in Mozart on the radio, driving somewhat sedately for him.

Still sore and subdued, I guess, I found I was glad to see familiar sights I hadn't even known I liked.

At a traffic light I watched an old woman bundled up in peasant clothes against the cold air. Her face and hands were cracked, red, and wrinkled from the weather. She sold fruit and nuts from a rickety wooden cart to a woman in Pucci pants whose Mercedes was idling at the corner. Behind her I could see the castle Prince Eugene of Savoy got for keeping the Turks out of Vienna in the seventeenth century. I wondered, somewhat cynically, whether he would have been so hot to keep out another invader, Adolf Hitler. Or whether he would have joined his fellow citizens dancing in the streets to welcome him. What a mixture this city was of old and new. Good and bad.

When we arrived home, the Goldbergs were there along with Branko, his wife, and the Martins. Frau Schnively leaned out of her window, her weight dangerously distributed on the overhang, and her tight little smile as disapproving as ever of foreigners.

Hannah and I winced at the hugs and reminded everyone of our still-sore muscles, but we didn't really mind.

"We have a feast to welcome you back," Mom said. "A

thanksgiving celebration for your safe return. Come on, every-one—into the dining room."

"Oh no! You didn't, Mom! Not for all these people. Not one of your gourmet dinners," I said, aghast.

"Very funny, son. I see your ordeal hasn't changed you much."

"I know," Nigel said. "But we got him back. You can't have everything, you know."

Now, I didn't see what was so funny about that, but every-one else seemed to.

"No, Con," Mom said. "I didn't do the cooking. Branko and Mrs. Goldberg are fully responsible. She taught him how to make the bagels. All I did was buy the pastrami and pickles."

We all stood together around the table, and Rev. Martin thanked God in that deep, strong voice of his for our safe return from the hands of evil men. And everyone there said "Amen!"

"All right! What are we waiting for, then?" Hannah said. "Let's eat."

And we did, till we were stuffed. We told our story in be-tween bagels.

"These bagels are very good, Branko," Nigel said. "But you know, you still can't make Viennese pastry like the Viennese, and you have been here fifty years. Don't you think it's a little late to start on Jewish breads?"

Branko's whole body shook with his quiet laugh. "You're right," he said. "I will leave that up to Frau Goldberg."

The phone rang, and I went to get it in the kitchen.

"That was Frau R.," I said upon returning to the dining room. "She just wanted to tell me to please try to stay out of trouble, at least until next weekend when she's coming for a visit. She also said that if I ever worry my parents like that again, I will have to answer to her."

"Good for her," Branko said, bringing out a special cake he had made for the occasion, a Sachertorte. Everyone oohed and ahhed and made room for more. "Also," Branko said, ignoring the praise, "the next time you kids spot a terrorist's car, don't hang around to take pictures. You understand?" At that moment he looked more like a bouncer than a baker, and I figured we should obey.

"Okay, okay, enough already. We get the point, don't we, Hannah?"

"Yeah, maybe—but we handled ourselves pretty well, you must admit," she said.

Even though we had talked to our moms on the phone for an hour from Zürich telling them the details, we went over the high points again.

"You should have heard Con's Abbott and Costello routine. He was extremely good," Hannah said flippantly, avoiding the heavy stuff.

"I admit it," Mom said. "I think both of you were clever and brave. You actually fooled those men, two of them, anyway. I'll sleep better knowing they're behind bars," she said with a shiver.

"But you know, without Nigel's insisting the police search for you right then, Dirty Harry would have gotten to you before the police did," Hannah's dad said, putting a dollop of whipped cream in his coffee. He went on to praise Nigel for his quick action.

Branko gave me a knowing look and whispered, "Pretty heroic, huh, Con?" I remembered our conversation about dads and smiled back at him.

Hannah's mother interrupted my thoughts and her husband's speech. "Enough of that. You are safely home now, and that is all that counts. Now it's time to get our heroine home for a good rest."

Hannah looked ready.

On the way out, Mr. Goldberg took me aside and said, "Con, Hannah told me over the phone what you said to those men. Standing with her, as it were."

He looked kindly at me, but his next words shocked me.

"It was a very dumb thing to do."

"I . . . I know, sir," I stammered, not expecting that. "I'm sorry."

"Well, don't be sorry," he said, giving me a bear hug. "It may have been dumb—but it was also a brave, noble thing to do."

With his hands on my shoulders, looking straight into my eyes, he told me why he thought so.

"All this about Donner has been terrible for you, and I understand that. You liked him, and it was a nasty shock to learn what he really was. But then when you saw the same thing in those men, you did what the majority of people failed to do during the Holocaust: You stood with the victim of that kind of irrational hatred. I'm proud of you and I thank you."

I didn't know what to say. I knew I didn't deserve his praise. I had acted on impulse more than reason. And it hadn't done Hannah any good. But her dad continued to speak.

"It seems to me that you've learned a lot in the last few days, and I think you deserve this. Anyway, our family would like you to have it." He took a small box out of his pocket and handed it to me.

Mom joined us in the hallway. She put her arm around my shoulder and smiled at me as I opened it. I had the feeling she knew what was in it.

I couldn't believe my eyes. It was another small, gold mezuzah, very much like Raoul's. I took out the little scroll. The Hebrew letters swam together before my eyes as I remembered with shame my feelings about Mom "using" my other one and the man who had given it to me only last Saturday.

It was very still in our little hallway. All the other voices seemed far away, and I didn't know what to say.

"Keep it. And remember," Mr. Goldberg said, sensing, I think, my emotions and inability to speak, "people like you and Hannah—the next generation—you must be the ones to see that it never happens again. Soon all the survivors will be gone, and then it will be easier for people to rewrite history and say the Holocaust never happened or that it wasn't any different from any other tragedy.

"If the message of Raoul's mezuzah is not forgotten, then his courageous effort will not have been in vain, even if Donner is never caught or punished. And remember, too, Con," Mr. Goldberg said, "if Donner hadn't given that mezuzah to you, Raoul's message would probably never have been read, certainly not in time to do what he wanted—condemn his murderer."

"Do you think we could find out if maybe Raoul was one of the few rescued from Graz?" Suddenly I wanted desperately for him to be alive, to be able to tell him we found the mezuzah.

"It is possible, of course," Mom answered me. "We can try to find out using the Documentation Center's files. But don't count on it, Con. You don't look for happy endings, because there were none in the Holocaust."

She had tears in her eyes. "Con, you played another role in this I haven't explained to you yet. It will only take a minute. I want Mr. Goldberg to hear it, too."

He nodded, and Mom said, "One day when you were still a baby, we visited the site of the concentration camp in Dachau. I had been reading and studying about the Holocaust, and after returning from Dachau, I had an argument with our local pastor, Rev. Neumüller. He had been giving me the standard excuses about people not knowing what was happening, the whole thing was exaggerated by Jewish activists, that kind of thing. I was beginning to study the real role, or lack of role, the church had played. But seeing the camp and talking with him must have made a huge impact, because that night I had a dream, which was really more like a vision. Nazi Storm Troopers broke into our apartment and beat you until blood covered your little blue sleeper, just like the one you really had on.

"They carried you through the streets of Grossgmain with me following after, screaming for you. Everyone in town stood by at their windows and in the streets, watching. No one helped me. Rev. Neumüller was there. He was wearing jackboots under his cleric robes, and he watched us go by. Then the gentle Catholic priest opened a door of the old church by the station, revealing the ornate, sculptured crucifix inside. Tacked to the door was a schedule of the week's events, decorated with a Nazi flag. At the train station they threw you into a sea of other children all crying for their mothers.

"I was awakened from that dream by our very own train passing through Grossgmain. I sat up the rest of the night holding you in my arms, thinking about all the mothers and fathers for whom the dream had been reality. Up until that time, I had been considering the Holocaust as something that happened to others. Shortly after my dream, I visited Wiesenthal and offered to do some work for him. In time my involvement doing investigative work for him grew. It took the experience of losing you, if only in a dream, to really get me involved. It shouldn't have."

"If only more people understood that," Mr. Goldberg said. "Whether the injustice is against the Jewish people or any other race, it is a problem for all of us."

"People often ask, 'Where was God during the Holocaust?' " Mom added. "I have heard it said and think it is true that the question is not 'Where was God,' but 'Where were God's people?' "

The ugly hatred of Knut and the others flashed before my eyes. My body was still sore from their blows. I ran my finger gently over a bruise on my face, thinking about what that same hatred had done when it ruled whole countries.

Mom felt me shiver and hugged me.

---◆---

Later that evening, when everyone had gone and we were alone, I asked Nigel to help me put my mezuzah on the doorframe of my room.

Mom got the tools and we nailed it up.

"Strictly against the rules," Nigel said, pounding in the nail. "Frau Schnively will charge me for this nail hole when we move out. Which might be soon, judging by her coolness since she learned of Roberta's involvement with Wiesenthal."

"Maybe she won't notice the hole," I said.

"Frau Schnively not notice?" He laughed. "Not jolly likely!"

After it was up, we all three sat on my bed looking at it, thinking our separate thoughts.

"What will happen to the other one, Mom?" I asked. "To Raoul's mezuzah?"

"What he wanted. It will be kept and used as evidence in Donner's trial as soon as they find him. Herr Wiesenthal is recovering and will be back at his work again soon, tracking down men like Donner, who may hide but can never rest as long as 'the hunter' is alive."

"Do you think they will? Find him, I mean?"

"I don't know, son. They might not. It's hard to say. The police finally moved in and searched the farmhouse where Frau Donner was staying. They found lots of interesting items, like two boxes full of things like your mezuzah. But no sign of Herr Donner. Frau Donner will only scream denials at the police—doesn't know where he got such things, has no idea where he is, and so on."

"What if they don't find him?"

"Then he will spend the rest of his life on the run." Mom sighed. "Money will be no object. The SS take care of their own. And there is a whole new generation of neo-Nazis in Austria and Germany. Unfortunately he will find refuge. But he will always be looking over his shoulder. That is a kind of punishment. And he can't ever go back to Grossgmain."

Looking over his shoulder . . . That's what I'd be doing if Dirty Harry ever got out of prison. I didn't much like the thought.

"Good," I said finally and meant it. I told her about Gregor's video game and confessed watching him play. Now I couldn't imagine how I could have watched or why his parents let him have it. "It was terrible," I said, still ashamed.

Mom shook her head sadly. "I know. A country that denies its past has trouble dealing with the present. Those video games are a good example. It makes me sad to think a little boy like Gregor could have one. Do you think his parents know?"

"Yes, they do. And he isn't a little boy, Mom. He's my age."

"Dead right," Nigel said, gazing at the mezuzah. "Little boy he most certainly is not.

"Well, I don't know about you two," Nigel went on, starting out the door, "but I have some work to get done before Monday morning."

"Thanks—Dad," I said.

He turned at that and looked at me, "Thanks for what, Con?"

"For—er—uh . . ." I couldn't find the right words to say how I had felt when that cabin door opened and it was him, not Harry, standing there. I knew he had tried as hard as any dad ever would to get his son back. I knew, but I didn't know how to say so. Instead, I said rather lamely, "Thanks for putting up my mezuzah."

"Why certainly, son," he said, knowing exactly what I meant. "Any time."

EPILOGUE

AN END

IT HAD BEEN ONLY SEVEN DAYS SINCE GROSSGMAIN, AND THE beginning of the end. But it seemed like another world. *I was just a kid this time last week*, I thought, and then I remembered the card Nigel had given me on my fifteenth birthday.

It was my first birthday as his son. The card had seemed kind of strange at the time, but I hadn't given it much thought. It was plain white with a black border on the outside. Inside Nigel had written in fancy script, *With sympathy—as childhood abates.*

I picked up the dictionary and looked up *abate*. "To súbside, to eliminate." Nigel's subtle humor hadn't made sense at the time. And he couldn't have known how prophetic his card was. But in one short week, my childhood had been eliminated. It had come to an end. Nothing would ever be the same.

I thought about Raoul and wondered what he was thinking when he carefully wrote his message in Hebrew and hid it in the mezuzah. Herr Donner had given me much more than evidence of his own guilt when he placed the mezuzah in my hands. He had made me face my own.

If Raoul had lived he might have gone to Israel, and Hannah or a girl like her could be his granddaughter. Hannah, my friend. She, like Raoul, would have been carried away to her death on one of the trains. The picturesque trains . . . the lulling sounds of which had put me to sleep night after night as they

195

rumbled through our mountain town. The priests and the preachers, the grocers, the farmers, and all the ordinary people had watched the trains and used them and made them come and go as they did years ago when the cargo was human and their destination death.

Love your neighbor as much as yourself. I wondered if I could. If I would.

I got up and looked out my window. Mom and Nigel had long since gone to bed, but I couldn't sleep. The courtyard looked like it was full of strange figures, bodies made of smoke creeping over the patio stones, writhing together while striving to rise. *Probably shadows in the moonlight*, I told myself, *moved about by rustling leaves.* But things are not always, maybe seldom, what they seem.

**Don't miss Con's next adventure
in PASSPORT TO DANGER!**

The Sagebrush Rebellion

Con leaves behind Vienna, Austria, his parents, and his best friend, Hannah, to head for the wilds of Wyoming, where he will spend his summer vacation with his grandparents and six girl cousins on the sprawling family ranch. Grandpa Walker has fallen ill, and the problems at the ranch haven't helped. Somebody's been cutting fences, and a number of cattle have mysteriously died.

Con and his cousins devise a scheme to find the culprit, but the list of suspects includes a radical environmental group, some local Native Americans, a jealous neighbor—and a famous movie star who's determined to buy Walker Ranch. As they investigate, the cousins discover the sabotage runs far deeper than they'd expected. Can they bring the truth to light before it's too late?

READING LIST

All But My Life by Gerda Weissmann Klein. New York: Hill & Wang, 1971.

> A story full of hope even during the worst despair. This amazing young Hungarian teenager survives concentration camps, the loss of her entire family, and a death march to eventually marry the American soldier who liberates her.

Anne Frank: The Diary of a Young Girl by Anne Frank. Garden City: Doubleday, 1952; Pocketbook, 1953, 1980.

> One of the most well-known and powerful documents of the Holocaust, her diary was found in the hiding place in Amsterdam where the family had hidden for two years. She died in Bergen-Belsen two months before Holland was liberated.

Anne Frank Remembered: The Story of the Woman Who Helped to Hide the Frank Family by Miep Gies. New York: Simon and Schuster, 1987.

> For more than two years, Miep and her husband helped hide Anne Frank and the others in the attic, risking their lives to bring food and news of the outside world into the secret annex.

Fragments of Isabella by Isabella Leitner. New York: Thomas A. Crowell, 1979.

> The story of a close-knit Hungarian Jewish family taken to Auschwitz in 1944 and how the five sisters give one

another courage to survive in a world run by Dr. Josef Mengele.

The Hiding Place by Corrie ten Boom. Various publishers.

The story of a Dutch woman who, with the help of her elderly father and sister, among others, protected Jews from the German death camps of World War II. She also retells her own experiences in prison camps.

Hitler's War Against the Jews: A Young Reader's Version by David Altschuler. New York: Behrman House, 1978.

Follows the growth of anti-Semitism in Germany from the sixteenth century through the Holocaust in the twentieth century.

I Never Saw Another Butterfly: Children's Drawings and Poems—Terezin, 1942–44. Ed. Hana Volawkova; trans. Jeanne Namcova. New York & London: McGraw Hill, 1971.

The majority of Terezin children perished; however, their artistic and literary legacy was preserved in these drawings, which were "allowed," and in the writings that were issued in secret.

Lest Innocent Blood Be Shed by Philip Hallie. New York: Harper & Row, 1979, 1980.

The story of a French Protestant village, led by their pastor, that sheltered hundreds of Jews and others who sought protection.

They Chose Life by Yehuda Bauer. New York: Institute of Human Relations of the American Jewish Committee and the Institute of Contemporary Jewry of Hebrew University, 1974.

A monograph of the Jewish resistance, for teachers to use with students.

Young Moshe's Diary: The Spiritual Torment of a Jewish Boy in Nazi Europe by Moshe Linker. Ed. Shaul Esh and Geoffrey Wigoder. Jerusalem: Yad Vashem and Board of Jewish Education, 1971.

Diary of a Dutch Orthodox teenager whose family lived under false papers for several years. It ends before he and his family are betrayed and sent to Auschwitz, where he perished.

The United States Holocaust Memorial Museum has educational materials available for teaching about the Holocaust. For more information, write or fax:

Resource Center for Educators
U.S. Holocaust Memorial Museum
100 Raoul Wallenberg Place SW
Washington, DC 20024–2150
FAX: (202) 488–6137

Young Adult Fiction Series From Bethany House Publishers
(Ages 12 and up)

CEDAR RIVER DAYDREAMS • by Judy Baer
Experience the challenges and excitement of high school life with Lexi Leighton and her friends.

GOLDEN FILLY SERIES • by Lauraine Snelling
Tricia Evanston races to become the first female jockey to win the sought-after Triple Crown.

JENNIE MCGRADY MYSTERIES • by Patricia Rushford
A contemporary Nancy Drew, Jennie McGrady's sleuthing talents bring back readers again and again.

LIVE! FROM BRENTWOOD HIGH • by Judy Baer
The staff of an action-packed teen-run news show explores the love, laughter, and tears of high school life.

PASSPORT TO DANGER • by Mary Reeves Bell
Constantine Rea, an American living in modern-day Austria, confronts the lasting horrors of the Holocaust.

THE SPECTRUM CHRONICLES • by Thomas Locke
Adventure awaits readers in this fantasy series set in another place and time.

SPRINGSONG BOOKS • by various authors
Compelling love stories and contemporary themes promise to capture the hearts of readers.

UNMISTAKABLY COOPER ELLIS • by Wendy Lee Nentwig
Laugh and cry with Cooper as she strives to balance modeling, faith, and life at her Manhattan high school.

WHITE DOVE ROMANCES • by Yvonne Lehman
Romance, suspense, and fast-paced action for teens committed to finding pure love.